EXPLORERS OF THE
NEW CENTURY

Also by Magnus Mills

The Scheme for Full Employment
Three to See the King
All Quiet on the Orient Express
The Restraint of Beasts

EXPLORERS OF THE NEW CENTURY

MAGNUS MILLS

A HARVEST ORIGINAL
HARCOURT, INC.
Orlando   Austin   New York   San Diego   Toronto   London

www.HarcourtBooks.com

First published in Great Britain by Bloomsbury Publishing Plc in 2005

Library of Congress Cataloging-in-Publication Data
Mills, Magnus.
Explorers of the new century/Magnus Mills.—1st U.S. edition.
p. cm.
"A Harvest Original."
1. Explorers—Fiction. I. Title.
PR6063.I37784E96 2006
823'.914—dc22 2005020987
ISBN-13: 978-0-15-603078-6 ISBN-10: 0-15-603078-0

Text set in Janson

Printed in the United States of America

First U.S. edition
A C E G I K J H F D B

For S. M. P.

EXPLORERS OF THE
NEW CENTURY

I

'HE'S A THOROUGHLY DECENT man,' said Johns. 'His reputation for fair play is second to none. Clearly he had good reason for his early departure and, therefore, we must allow him the benefit of the doubt. It goes without saying that this development will have no bearing on our own arrangements. We'll continue with our preparations and proceed as per schedule.'

'But he's stolen a march on us!' protested Summerfield.

'That doesn't matter,' replied Johns. 'We're not in a competition to see who gets there first, and I don't want anyone thinking in those terms. What concerns us now is the immediate job in hand. How long do you reckon till nightfall, Scagg?'

'About an hour.'

'Right you are then. The temperature is already beginning to plummet, so we'd better get the stove fired up. Then we'll see about getting some supplies landed.' Johns glanced around the blockhouse. 'I must say they've left this place in immaculate condition. Quite spick and span. One would never think it was occupied until only a few days ago.'

'They've even replenished the coal stocks,' said Scagg.

'Yes indeed. They were obviously expecting us to arrive hard on their heels. Well, we might as well make the most of their kindness. Can you light a fire, Summerfield?'

'Yes I can.'

'All right. See to it, will you? The rest of us can set to work unloading the *Centurion*.' Johns turned and led the way outside, followed by most of the others. Only Summerfield and Plover remained behind. They stood gazing at the stove, then Plover laid his hand on the iron plate.

'Stone cold,' he said. 'This hasn't been lit for at least a week.'

'As long as that?' asked Summerfield.

'At the very least. And I don't care what Johns says about fair play: in my opinion they cleared out of here at the first opportunity.'

'Leaving a barrel of coal in recompense.'

'Quite.'

The door opened and Scagg looked in. 'Two to light a fire, gentlemen?'

'We were just talking a moment,' said Plover.

'So I see.'

Scagg said nothing more, but waited in silence as Summerfield bent quickly to his task. Meanwhile, Plover buttoned his reefer, thrust his hands in his pockets, and went outside.

The blockhouse stood on a low headland. Down by the water's edge, a number of boxes, sacks and crates were being unloaded from the cutter. Two men sat at the oars, and as soon as everything was beached they rowed back out to the anchorage for further supplies. On Scagg's instructions, Plover went and assisted Johns. The mules had been roped together and swum ashore, and Johns was examining them one by one as they recovered their land legs.

'We'll put them in the lee of the blockhouse after they've had some hot mash,' he announced, when Plover joined him. 'They'll need a while to acclimatise after so many days at sea. Perhaps you could rig up some kind of shelter; a tarpaulin slung across poles maybe?'

'I'll see what I can do,' said Plover.

'Very good.'

Johns completed his appraisal, then the two of them stood for some minutes regarding the mules, which had now gathered in a group, their ropes slack as they huddled together for warmth.

'They're in pretty good condition for the most part,' Johns remarked at length. 'We won't work them for the time being, though. They've got a rough time ahead, and we need to conserve their strength.'

'Shall I see Seddon for some equipment?' Plover asked.

'Yes,' said Johns. 'I've appointed him as quartermaster, so tell him what you need and that will be all right. Now I need to go and speak with Scagg.'

'I'm thinking of offering the men a choice this evening. To mark our last day at sea they can have the option of either staying on board the *Centurion* for one more night, or else sleeping in the blockhouse. It will be entirely up to them. Personally, I'm very happy to be back on terra firma, but I know it's likely to be a wrench for some.'

'They'll have to get used to it soon enough,' said Scagg.

'You're quite right,' replied Johns. 'Nevertheless, I think they'll appreciate the gesture. Could you see your way to passing the word around?'

'As you wish, Mr Johns. Was there anything else?'

'Not at present, no. You appear to have everything running smoothly. I expect you could do with an extra pair of hands, though?'

'It would help.'

'Very well,' said Johns. 'I'm at your disposal until dusk.'

'Oh, I didn't mean . . .'

'It's all right, Scagg. Every one of us is going to have to put his shoulder to the wheel if this expedition's to be a success. Now what would you like me to do?'

'Well, the cutter is just coming back, so that will need unloading.'

'Right you are. Leave it to me.'

'Thank you, sir.'

Scagg watched as Johns trudged across the sand to meet the boat. Then he went and found Cook, who was busy lashing down a stack of crates. 'When you've finished doing that, go and give Mr Johns some help,' Scagg ordered. 'And don't let him get his feet wet.'

The rest of the day's work was straightforward: a simple matter of bringing in as many supplies as possible before dark. Actually, no one ceased from their labours until night had crept fully on to the shore and was beginning to hamper further progress. Only then did Scagg call everyone into the blockhouse for supper. Johns returned in his own time, having carried out a cursory inspection of the camp. When at last he went inside he was met by a general cheer from the men. A bottle had been opened to celebrate their landing, and as they gathered around the stove he spelt out his plans for the following day.

'We've made excellent advances so far,' he began. 'If we continue at the same rate, we'll have all our provisions ashore by noon tomorrow. Then, tide permitting, I want to see about getting the *Centurion* beached. Will your estimates allow for that, Chase?'

'Should be all right, Mr Johns.'

'Good. It's going to be hard work, there's no avoiding that, but we'll travel easier knowing that the ship's safe. In the meantime I suggest an early night. Your various tasks will be posted at daybreak.' Johns paused and looked around him. 'By the way, where are Blanchflower and Firth?'

'They've opted to stay on board this evening,' said Scagg. 'I've told them to bring in the cutter at first light.'

'Fully laden, I hope?'

'Of course, sir. Blanchflower knows what we need.'

'Well, Scagg, you seem to have everything organised so I'm going to turn in now, if nobody minds. I'll take one of the upper bunks. Good night, everyone, and congratulations: we've trodden our first few steps.'

Johns was cheered again as he ascended the ladder to bed. Then, while the men quietly resumed their supper, he made an entry in his journal:

Tostig has struck for the interior. We will follow in due course.

At dawn, a greenish bloom arose in the eastern sky, spreading gradually into a vast gleaming radiance. As darkness receded, Cook emerged from the blockhouse and grimaced at the sea. Closing the door behind him, he swiftly unfolded Johns's standard, ran it up the flagpole and secured it. Then he went inside again. A little while later smoke began issuing from the chimney. At about the same time, Blanchflower appeared on the foredeck of the *Centurion*. He looked across at the standard flapping stiffly in the breeze, and immediately went below to wake Firth.

Now Medleycott opened the blockhouse door and stood gazing out. Within seconds someone inside demanded that he shut it right away, so he did as they asked before wandering down to the water's edge. On the horizon, the early light was giving way to a cold greyness. Medleycott picked up a flat pebble and skimmed it into the waves. Then Blanchflower and Firth started moving around on the *Centurion*. Medleycott watched as they lowered some boxes into the cutter, climbed aboard and cast off.

"'Each man should try to do an hour's work before breakfast,'" said a voice behind him.

He turned round and saw Plover coming down the beach.

'Yes,' said Medleycott. 'I noticed that when I was reading through the postings. Quite a smart idea really. Good morning, by the way.'

'Morning,' replied Plover. 'I assume it's Johns' method of ensuring we all build up a healthy appetite.'

'Yes.'

'As if we wouldn't in a place like this.'

'Well, I think anything that gets us on the move can

only be to our advantage,' offered Medleycott. 'After all, the sooner we get the work done, the sooner we can get going inland.'

'I suppose so.'

'Better look sharp. Here's Scagg.'

The cutter was now halfway to the shore, so the two of them got into the surf and made ready to catch it as it came in. At the same time, Scagg came down from the blockhouse, followed by Seddon, Chase and Cook. The provisions were quickly landed, then relayed on to higher ground. With Scagg directing operations, the cutter underwent three more journeys during that first part of the day, and by mid-morning all the portable equipment had been stashed near the blockhouse. After breakfast, Johns asked Scagg if he could 'borrow' Chase for an hour or so. Scagg obliged, and the pair went off to conduct a brief coastal survey. Meanwhile, the *Centurion* was prepared for beaching. Around midday, lines were taken out and made secure. Next the ballast was discharged and the vessel allowed to float in on the tide. Plover and Summerfield had harnessed the mules in readiness; these were now brought down to the water's edge. Then the *Centurion* was gradually hauled ashore, with the entire crew helping the mules cover the last few yards. Johns and Chase returned just in time to lend a hand, taking their place on the ropes alongside the others. Finally, timber supports were positioned beneath the hull, and tarpaulins fastened over to protect it from the weather.

Further along the shore, about half a mile to the east, a second ship lay already beached. The bulk of the day's work having been completed, Johns ordered a break. Then he and Scagg walked over to have a look at the other vessel. It was a converted steam tug, similar to their own though slightly shorter in length, carrying the name *Perseverance*. Painted blue with yellow gunwales (the *Centurion* was red and white), it stood clasped in a makeshift wooden cradle, fully battened down, with sand gathering slowly around its keel.

'Very thorough work,' said Johns, testing a guy line for tautness. 'Not a loose fitting to be seen.'

'He certainly hasn't left anything to chance,' remarked Scagg.

'Each item in its proper place, just as I'd expect. And would you believe he's even stuck a marker post at the beginning of his trail? Chase and I discovered it when we were out surveying this afternoon.'

'So you know the route he's taken?'

'Well, we're fairly certain,' replied Johns. 'As far as we can tell, he's gone by way of that dry river bed we could see as we sailed in yesterday.'

'But wasn't that your preferred direction, sir?'

Johns smiled. 'Initially, yes, Scagg. However, it seems to me that there's little to be gained from two parties treading the same ground. Indeed, it may prove favourable to establish a secondary, alternative route. With this in mind, I've decided we'll take a more westerly path than that chosen by Tostig.'

'The river bed looks the easier way by far,' Scagg pointed out. 'The natural course is often the best.'

'Maybe so,' Johns smiled again. 'But I'm sure our journey will be much more interesting.'

At that moment a cry went up from the main work party. This was followed by a commotion around the *Centurion*. Quickly they hurried back, and were met halfway by Plover. They paused briefly to hear his news.

'I'm afraid there's been a mishap.'

'What happened?' asked Scagg.

'Well, a few of us decided to drive some extra wedges under the hull. To make it more secure, so we thought.'

'Who's this "we"?'

'A few of us.'

'And?'

'Unfortunately, we overdid it and the boat tipped forward. One of the mules was crushed under the port bow.'

'What?!' bellowed Scagg, quickly starting off once more. Johns said nothing, but followed with the others to where the hapless creature lay trapped. It was still attached to the rest of the mules, which were now being unharnessed and carefully led away by Summerfield and Firth. Scagg observed the scene for some moments before rounding on Plover.

'Why hadn't they been moved clear?!' he demanded. 'And what was the idea of adding more wedges without consulting myself or Mr Johns?!'

Plover did not reply.

'Well?' said Scagg.

As Plover stood before them, seemingly unable to answer, Johns at last broke his silence.

'It doesn't matter, Scagg,' he said.

'But it's such a waste, sir!'

'I know, I know. Yet whatever happened was plainly an

accident, and doubtless a valuable lesson has been learned as a result. We'll just have to make do with one less mule, that's all.'

From his pocket he produced a revolver, which he loaded and handed to Scagg. Scagg passed it to Cook, who walked over and quickly destroyed the mule. Then Johns turned and addressed the men in general. 'Could everyone please try to be a little more careful in future? I should hate us to lose another.'

'Sorry for my part in that,' murmured Plover.

'That's all right,' Johns replied. 'Now perhaps a few of us could get this boat straightened out and made safe again. Can you see the best way of going about it, Scagg?'

'Well, I dare say we'll manage something if we give it a bit of thought.'

'Good.'

'And the mule will need burying.'

'Of course.'

'So if you want to leave it with me, Mr Johns? I'm sure you've got more important issues to deal with.'

'All right, Scagg. Thank you. Yes, I could do with consulting Chase again to discuss possible routes. Maybe we'll have another stroll before dark.'

'Marvellous!' said Cook. 'Sheets, pillows and a mattress. Makes a change from swinging about in that blasted hammock.'

'Well, you'd better make the most of it,' remarked Sargent. 'Once we set off inland you'll have to get by with your utility blanket and nothing more.'

Cook stretched himself and yawned. 'Yes, I'm fully aware of that fact, thank you,' he said. 'But I'll worry about sacrifice and hardship when we've received the order to move, and not a moment before.'

'There'll be no luxury of any kind,' Sargent continued. 'No hot-water bottles. No thickly buttered toast. No orange marmalade or lemon curd. And no more bedtime cocoa.'

'No cocoa? Whyever not?'

'Because we'll be getting a patent malt drink instead.'

'Good grief.'

'My thoughts exactly. I've heard it's made with powdered milk.'

'How do they produce that then?'

'I've no idea, but apparently Johns swears by it. Brought a whole crateful with us.'

'Must be one of his "innovations".'

'Yes, I suppose so.'

Rolling out of his bunk, Cook padded over to the stove. 'Oh well, if it helps keep the blinking cold out I'll give anything a try. I heard the mercury dropped to fifteen below last night.'

'That's nothing,' said Sargent. 'We'll be losing the sun in a week or two. Then we'll really know about it. Put some fuel in there, will you?'

'All right.'

In the corner stood a coal bucket, which Cook grabbed and swung upwards, emptying the contents into the stove. He did this in a careless manner, allowing black dust to spill on to the floor. Closing the lid, he adjusted the flame before seizing a broom to sweep up. Sargent, meanwhile, had pulled a sheet from his bunk and was giving it a shake.

The door opened and Scagg looked in. 'Spring cleaning, gentlemen?'

'Not really, no,' Cook answered.

'What are you doing then?'

'Nothing.'

'Why not?'

'We thought it was a rest day,' said Sargent. 'There was no work posted this morning.'

'That's because you're supposed to be carrying out voluntary tasks.'

'Well, no one told us.'

'You shouldn't have needed telling!' declared Scagg. 'Mr Johns expects people to just get on with things without being "told". At the moment, for example, Blanchflower and Firth are outside this very blockhouse, applying a new coat of whitewash. Summerfield's helping Medleycott gather driftwood, and Seddon's gone out in the cutter to see if he can catch some fish.'

'What about Plover?' enquired Cook. 'What's he doing?'

Scagg came inside, closed the door, and spoke with a lowered voice. 'Don't concern yourselves about Plover,' he said. 'I'm keeping my beady eye on him, you can be sure of that. But for your own sakes get on with something useful. You don't want Mr Johns to catch you slacking, do you?'

'Of course not.'

'Well then.' Scagg glanced at the stove. 'Tell you what, why don't you bring in the rest of the coal?'

'All right,' said Cook. 'Can we have a bit of breakfast first?'

'Certainly you can.'

'Like some?'

'No thanks. I had mine hours ago.'

By this time, Sargent had finished making his bed. He tucked in the final corner, then turned round to face Scagg. 'Don't mind my asking,' he said. 'But when are we going to get moving?'

'As soon as the survey's complete,' Scagg replied. 'Could be tomorrow; could be the day after.'

'But all the time we spend here Tostig's forging ahead.'

'That has nothing to do with us. Mr Johns won't hear of leaving until he's got the full lie of the land. I'm afraid you're going to have to be patient, that's all.'

'Well, I only hope he knows what he's doing.'

'Of course he knows what he's doing!' Scagg snapped. 'Now get on with your work and don't let's have so much of it!'

He marched outside, slamming the door behind him. This caused the flames briefly to flare up inside the stove. Cook glanced at Sargent and shrugged. 'You'd better be careful what you say to him in future.'

'All right I will, but I must say I don't like the sound of all this volunteering for extra work.'

'I suppose it's meant to be a chance for us to show willing.'

'But we volunteered to come on this trip, didn't we? Wasn't that showing willing enough?'

'Well, to be truthful, I don't really mind getting the rest of the coal in. It'll only take an hour or so, the two of us together.'

'That's not the point,' replied Sargent. 'If the job needed doing then someone should have said!'

On the evening before the journey began, Scagg went out alone. Sometime after supper he slipped unnoticed from the blockhouse, crossed the headland, and began walking westward. The moon was down. There were no landmarks along that deserted coast; no trees or bushes; and only a few stars to light his way. From time to time he paused to glance at the sea, or to pick up a stone whose shape caught his interest. This he would examine momentarily in the gloom, before casting it aside and continuing again in the same direction. Eventually he came to the dry river bed, where he headed inland, following its course between gradually rising banks. After another minute he arrived at a thin wooden pole stuck into the ground. At the top fluttered a small pennant. Here Scagg halted and stood for a long while gazing into the darkness beyond. Then he turned and retraced his steps back to the blockhouse. Inside, all was quiet. He opened the door and saw Johns sitting by the stove.

'Ah, Scagg,' he said. 'Just in time for "lights out".'

The rest of the party had retired for the evening, though none of them were yet asleep. They lay on their bunks writing diaries, or making minor preparations for the days ahead, replacing lost buttons and so forth. Only after Johns said good night did they try and get their heads down, but even then few slumbered properly. There was much to do next day, and long before dawn the whole company was up and about once more.

Cook had been instructed not to raise the flag that morning, and instead his first duty was to make some boiled mash for the mules. They were to be given extra portions to nourish them for the arduous journey that lay ahead, though Cook was careful not to be too generous.

'Don't want them getting fat,' he muttered to himself, as he carried the steaming pot round to the rear of the blockhouse.

Meanwhile, his companions busied themselves with sundry tasks, getting the supplies ready for carrying and making sure nothing had been forgotten. The hour's work before breakfast passed quickly. Then, when everyone came outside again, Johns asked them to gather round him.

'So we have,' he said, reading from a list, 'Blanchflower, Chase, Cook, Firth, Medleycott, Plover, Sargent, Seddon and Summerfield. All present, Scagg?'

'All present, Mr Johns.'

'Very good. Now it's far too cold to stand here making speeches. I've no time for such flummery, so without further ado I think we'll make an immediate start. I just want to say, however, that I believe you have all been well chosen. I could not wish to begin an expedition such as this with a finer set of fellows. In Chase, for instance, we have one of the best navigators of our age. As you know, his excellent guidance brought the *Centurion* to this forsaken shore without a single fault, and I am relying fully on his judgment over the coming weeks as we head for the interior. Likewise, I regard Scagg as a most able deputy, and if anything should happen to me he will, of course, take command. As for the rest of you, well you are competent individuals without exception. You all know where we're going and why we're going there. It may take a good while, but I am confident that we'll achieve our goal as long as each of us pulls in the same direction. Now, Scagg, the blockhouse has been left in a fit state, I presume?'

'Yes, Mr Johns. Everything's in order.'

'All right then. Lock the door, will you, and we'll go.'

During the past few days Johns had taken to wearing his woolly helmet, a practice swiftly adopted by the majority of the party. Plover, alone, persisted in sporting a high-peaked cap. The rest of the men, their faces hidden, could easily be distinguished from one another by their various gaits as they began their long march. The twenty-three mules, now fully laden, were led in train by Blanchflower and Firth, with the remainder of the group following in the rear. Johns was 'last man'. He paused for a moment to gaze out to sea, and then, after a final glance at his ship, he set off in pursuit.

The leading mules were over the headland and on to the vague trail that had been established as far as the dry river bed. When Johns caught up, he sent Chase forward to help conduct them to the other side. It was an easy crossing, during which not one member of the party drew attention to the pennant fluttering on its pole a hundred yards inland. Instead, they all helped drive the mules up the far bank and on to the start of the 'westerly' route.

'The wind has swung ahead,' observed Chase, as they regained level ground. 'We're going straight into it.'

'Well, it can't be helped,' Johns answered. 'Doubtless it will swing back round in due course.'

'Mr Johns!' called a voice from the rear. 'Mr Johns, could I have a word?!'

Johns turned to see Medleycott coming up the slope. Beyond him were Cook and Sargent, who had paused briefly to adjust their packs.

'Certainly, Medleycott. What is it?'

'I was wondering . . .' Medleycott waited a few moments to allow Chase to move slightly ahead. 'Has anyone mentioned the tents?'

'No, they haven't,' replied Johns. 'Good gracious! Are you telling me we've left them behind?'

'No, no,' said Medleycott. 'We've brought all four. I made sure and loaded them myself.'

'What's the matter then?'

'It's just that I wondered if there were any plans. About who's going to be put with who.'

'You mean the allocation of places?'

'Yes.'

'It's been taken care of. As far as I recall, there are three to a tent apart from myself and Scagg. He's organised it all.'

'Oh.'

'So I'm afraid you'll need to speak with him if you wish to know who you're sharing with.'

'And it's set in granite, is it?'

'I really don't know, Medleycott, but this isn't the time or place to discuss such matters. What exactly are those two fiddling about with back there?'

'I think they're tightening their straps.'

'Well, let's hope they make an effort to catch up soon. We've only been on the move for half an hour and already the party's becoming strung out. The last thing I want is for everyone to divide into separate little groups all going at different speeds. That would be terribly harmful to the expedition, so please let's try and keep together, can we?'

'Yes, of course, Mr Johns. Sorry for the delay.'

'And I'm sure you'll be perfectly all right, whichever tent you're in.'

'Thank you.'

Without a further word, Medleycott put his head down and pressed forward. After another minute he had latched on to the main group, where there was little talking to be heard. Each of the men walked in silence, leaning into the wind and settling to an even pace as the untrodden land opened up before them. Only Summerfield journeyed alone. Having already moved clear of the mules, he could now be seen as a remote figure, leading the way towards a chain of distant blue hills.

'Impatient as ever,' commented Chase, when Medleycott drew alongside him. 'If he keeps going at that rate we'll lose sight of him altogether.'

'He knows where he's going, does he?' Medleycott enquired.

'I've given him a rough bearing, yes, though to tell you the truth he can hardly go wrong. It's steady as she goes until we can see the best way through those hills. Or over them.'

'What do you think is on the other side?'

'Who knows? More of the same, I'd hazard.'

'A desolate region bereft of life.'

'That's very well put,' said Chase.

'I've spotted one or two dwarf plants along the way, and the occasional tuft of grass, but little else. Nothing to suggest some verdant belt lying just around the corner.'

'No.'

The conversation was difficult to sustain, held as it was in the face of the wind, and perpetually muffled by their woolly helmets. Nonetheless, Medleycott persisted.

'I don't suppose,' he asked, 'if you've heard who's going in which tent?'

'No, I haven't,' replied Chase. 'Why, was there someone with whom you especially wished to share?'

'No, there wasn't.'

'So it's someone you'd rather not share with?'

'It's neither.'

'Then it barely matters, does it? As long as you get some shelter, that's all that counts.'

'Yes, I suppose you're right,' said Medleycott. 'I was just interested really.'

'Now I wonder what's stopped him in his tracks?'

By this time Summerfield was almost a mile ahead of them, but they could see that he had come to an abrupt halt.

'Maybe he's resting,' suggested Medleycott.

'Possibly,' Chase answered, pausing to gaze into the distance. 'But, knowing Summerfield, he'd be more likely to press on until he reached a definite point. He wouldn't just stop halfway.'

They watched as Summerfield turned and made his way back towards them. Then he halted again, seemingly unable to make up his mind. For a few seconds more he continued to hesitate, before finally turning again and carrying on in the original direction. His speed of movement, though, appeared somewhat slower than it had been before.

'Perhaps he's giving the rest of us a chance to catch up,' said Plover, who had now joined Chase and Medleycott. Chase glanced at him but said nothing in reply, then the three of them resumed their headlong march. Only after another twenty minutes did they discover the cause of Summerfield's apparent indecision. Until now the ground they'd been travelling on had consisted of hard bare earth, rough in places but generally firm underfoot. All of a sudden, however, it began to change, the earth quickly vanishing under an immense sweep of pebbles that stretched ahead as far as they could see. The leading mules had already got on to the new surface, and were clearly finding it a hindrance to their progress. Meanwhile, Summerfield continued pushing forward, the margin now reduced to about half a mile. With careful tread, the others followed.

'"Some of the seeds fell on stony ground,"' remarked Plover, before being pulled up by Scagg.

'Wait a moment everybody!' he called. 'I want to speak to Mr Johns before we go any further.'

The whole party took the opportunity to rest while Scagg went back to meet Johns.

'What is it, Scagg?' he asked.

'Scree,' Scagg replied. 'Mile upon mile of it, rising all the way to those hills, from what I can make out.'

'Is there any way round it?'

'Unfortunately not. It's covering our path completely.'

Johns peered beyond his second-in-command, his eyes studying the vast stretch of wilderness.

'Who's that man up ahead?' he enquired at length.

'Summerfield,' Scagg answered. 'He's been blazing the trail.'

'Well, he seems to be making reasonable headway,' Johns announced. 'So I propose we carry on. After all, we can hardly allow every obstacle we meet to turn us aside.'

'Very well, Mr Johns. I just thought I'd better consult with you before we ventured too far.'

'Yes, that's all right, Scagg. Tell the men to take a short break, then we'll get moving again before we lose our momentum. And I must have a quiet word with Summerfield when I get the chance. His enthusiasm is laudable, but I think we need to rein him in a little at this early stage. Otherwise heaven knows what he might lead us into.'

Summerfield did, in fact, appear to have noticed that the main party had come to a halt. He could be seen in the distance, standing at the start of a gentle slope, his pack resting on the ground while he awaited his companions. The mules, likewise, were motionless. They stood patiently in a long line, one behind the other.

When the journey restarted, a change was immediately noticeable. Not only was the going much slower than it had been before, but now each man's step was accompanied by the harsh crunch of stones beneath his feet.

This sound was to accompany them relentlessly during their entire time on the scree.

Johns insisted that henceforth a tighter formation should be adopted, 'in order to prevent anyone straying too far behind or ahead', as he put it. It was decided that this was best achieved by having all the men travel forward of the mule train, so as to set a steady pace.

'You can't tell a mule how fast to go,' murmured Cook to Sargent when they reshouldered their packs. 'They've only got one speed, and that's their own.'

Medleycott overheard the comment. 'If you've got reservations,' he said, 'why don't you voice them to Johns instead of just muttering darkly?'

'Because it's got nothing to do with me,' Cook replied. 'My opinions don't count.'

'But surely it's your duty to speak out.'

Cook gazed at Medleycott and shook his head. 'There's no need. It'll be obvious soon enough.'

For the next half hour they advanced two by two across the scree, and good progress was recorded. Yet the further they went the deeper the layers of stone became, causing an increased degree of drag. Moreover, the gradient was uneven in places, with the ground falling away to one side or the other, so that the men were often obliged to walk in single file. Maintaining any sort of close form-ation was also impeded by the sheer physical differences between individuals, and it was not long before the idea was abandoned in all but name. Summerfield, meanwhile, continued to forge ahead, having started forward the moment the main party began moving again. No one had been able to communicate Johns's instructions to him, so they could do nothing but watch as his bobbing form gradually faded into the distance. It was becoming clear that what they'd assumed to be hills were mere peaks in this great pebbly expanse. It rolled away from them in a series of crests, swept ceaselessly by the unremitting wind. Another stop was called to allow an extra layer of clothing to be donned. At the same time some food and drink was taken.

'I'm afraid these delays are unavoidable for the present,' Johns observed. 'But I should think we can reduce their frequency once we've properly settled into our stride.'

He was sitting alongside Scagg and Chase, all three with their backs to the wind, facing the way they'd come. For reasons of his own, Scagg had rolled his woolly helmet upwards to form a sort of cap, so that only his ears and crown were protected from the cold. He now showed the beginnings of a beard.

'I hope Summerfield realises,' he said, 'that we'll be needing to make camp at some stage. The light will only last another hour and a half at the most.'

'I imagine he'll start looking for somewhere suitable fairly soon,' Johns replied.

'Well, it'll be at the foot of a leeward slope, if he's got any sense. Shall I give the signal to resume then?'

'Yes, if you will, Scagg.'

During that first part of the journey the sky had remained a uniform grey, with only a faint gleam at the horizon to indicate the presence of the sun. As the afternoon progressed, however, the gleam reddened, suggesting they could expect a brighter day tomorrow. In a long, final haul they traversed a broad ridge of particularly loose stones, to be confronted with yet another ridge about a mile away. In between there lay a shallow depression, and at its lowest point waited Summerfield. The sight of the continuing scree produced an audible groan from some members of the party. This seemed not to be heard by Johns, who had already begun his descent, but nevertheless it brought a rebuke from Scagg.

'Any more of that whingeing,' he growled, 'and you'll all be going to bed early without supper.'

The mood lightened considerably the moment they dipped out of the wind. The depression was a gloomy spot, and a difficult place to pitch tents, but the shelter it offered brought general agreement that it was a good choice. Summerfield was congratulated by Chase, who was first to join him, followed soon after by Medleycott and Seddon. When everyone had arrived, Scagg ordered the unloading of the tents. 'All right,' he said, referring to his notebook. 'Chase: you'll be with Blanchflower and Firth tonight. Seddon, Plover and Summerfield: you can all team up together. I'll be sharing with Mr Johns. That leaves Cook, Sargent and Medleycott. I suggest you keep the tents as close to one another as possible to maintain some warmth. Then we'll have some food please, Seddon.'

This being the first occasion the tents had been unpacked since coming ashore, it took a little trial and error to get them properly erected, especially as they could not be pegged down. Instead, they had to be weighted with stones, and by the time the work was finished a couple of lamps needed to be lit. Meanwhile, a field kitchen had been set up, complete with spirit stove, from which Seddon produced an evening meal. This was later described by Johns as 'miraculous', and earned Seddon a hearty three cheers. Afterwards Plover went over and offered to help him put away the cooking equipment. Everyone else had retired to their allotted tents, and the only sounds were the muted conversations coming from within. Johns could be seen in silhouette at his camp table, writing his journal by lamplight. Summerfield was already asleep. Plover gathered together a group of nestling pans, then spoke quietly to Seddon.

'You've heard what Medleycott's been doing, have you?'

'No, I haven't,' Seddon replied. 'I've been too busy.'

'He's been going round all day asking people which tents they're in.'

'Well, he didn't ask me.'

'As a matter of fact he didn't ask me either,' said Plover. 'But apparently he's made quite an issue of it. Even spoke to Johns himself. Not that he's gained anything for all his troubles: he's still ended up stuck with Cook and Sargent.'

During this exchange, Seddon had been folding away a large canvas windbreak. Now he stood up and glared at Plover.

'Meaning what?' he asked.

'What?' said Plover.

'What do you mean "stuck with Cook and Sargent"?'

'Well . . . you know.'

'No, I don't know!' Seddon snapped. 'Look, Plover, I'm not interested in your gossip, so can you just get on and hand me those pans if you're going to?!'

'All right, all right.'

'And if you really mean to help me you could at least stop getting in my way.'

They completed the rest of the chores in silence, before returning to their shared tent. Seddon entered first, taking care not to wake Summerfield as he did so. Plover stayed outside for a while longer, and added a few extra stones to those already piled along the edges. Then he, too, went to bed.

When Summerfield emerged at first light, he noticed that something had disturbed the mules. They were in an agitated state, straining on their tethers, heads all turned in the same direction. As they pressed against one another, each jostling for an advantage, he tried to follow their line of vision. For a moment there appeared a remote glint, perhaps ten miles away to the north-east, and again the mules kicked up. Summerfield blinked and peered once more into the distance, but he saw nothing else. Speaking softly to his charges, he now made a big show of measuring out the quantities for their hot mash, and getting the pot ready. His actions had the desired pacifying effect. Within a few minutes the mules had settled down to a calm anticipation of breakfast. Leaving the pot to boil, Summerfield then set off across the scree towards the next crest. It was more steeply inclined than the previous one, rising quickly to a sharp ridge, which he reached after a quarter of an hour's hard scrambling. When he made the top his eyes were met by a further vast tract of monotonous stony ground. The oncoming wind had not abated.

Pausing only long enough to take a deep breath, Summerfield turned and headed back.

In his absence, the other members of the party had risen and were all occupied making preparations for the day's march.

'I really must have a word with Summerfield,' Johns remarked, when he was spotted moving around on the ridge. 'It's all very well him scouting ahead all the time, but if he's not careful he's going to expend all his energy before we get anywhere.'

'Do you want me to speak to him?' asked Scagg.

'No, it's all right, thank you, Scagg,' said Johns. 'It only requires a gentle word.'

'Gentle word, my Aunt Molly,' declared Cook. He'd been working near to Johns and Scagg, and had overheard their discussion. A short while later, as he and Sargent packed their tent, he gave forth his own particular opinion. 'It was Summerfield's blessed fault we got on to this scree in the first place. If he'd only given Johns a chance to make a decision we could have done a detour; gone round the side or whatever it demanded, instead of ploughing straight through the middle. That was the worst night I've ever had, lying on all those blinking stones. I never slept a wink.'

'Why were you snoring so much then?' asked Sargent.

'Who was?'

'You were. You kept waking me up. And Medleycott.'

'Well, Medleycott can hardly complain about me. He spent half an hour folding his clothes away before he put the light out.'

'He didn't complain.'

'Oh.'

'Shared his chocolate with us, actually.'

'Yes, I'll give him that,' conceded Cook. 'He did share his chocolate.'

By the time they left Summerfield's Depression, as the site had now been named, the sun was already partway through its slow crawl along the southern horizon. It appeared as a dull red orb, offering little in the way of warmth, and providing light for only a few short hours. Faced with this scarcity, they continued travelling in a straight line.

'We can assume,' said Johns, 'that the terrain is bound to change eventually.'

2

'WHY HAS HE TURNED it into such a struggle?' said Tostig. 'We've established a perfectly good trail along our river bed, clearly marked at frequent intervals, yet for some reason he has to go and take a different route altogether. Completely unnecessary.'

'Maybe he's trying to make a race of it,' said Guthrum.

'You think so?'

'The evidence certainly suggests he is.'

'Indeed it does, Guthrum, indeed it does. So that's his game, eh? All right then: if it's a race he wants he can damn well have one!'

Tostig raised his field glasses and continued to watch as the distant, tiny figures inched across the scree. 'Eleven men,' he said. 'And two dozen mules. Roughly two dozen. Far more than he needs, I would have thought, unless he's counting on heavy losses.'

'He's making very good speed,' Guthrum remarked. 'That surface must be hell to travel on.'

'I'm not surprised at all,' answered Tostig. 'They're a wayfaring people, just as we are, and a stretch of slow-going won't daunt their spirits. Hardship means nothing to them.'

'Will you tell the others we have a rival?'

'Yes, of course. They should be informed at once. Come on.'

Without a further word the two men turned and made their way down from their viewpoint. They had been standing on a natural abutment that rose up on one side of the dry watercourse. Below them, on the sandy bed, their three companions were breaking camp. The river had narrowed considerably since the start of the journey; its meanderings were frequent; and its arid banks had crumbled in many places. Nonetheless, it persisted in providing a ready-made route inland. Tostig's passage, thus far, had been an easy one. Now, on his return, he had an announcement to make.

'Johns and his party have finally made an appearance,' he began. 'We've just sighted them about twelve miles to our west, cutting directly across an area of scree. We're still ahead of them but it's clear they've gained substantial ground. Whether they'll be able to sustain their progress is another matter entirely. From what we can make out, they are transporting a huge amount of supplies and equipment, so I think we can safely assume that this is more than a half-hearted sortie. It's plain that Johns and Company mean business.'

Tostig paused and allowed his men a few moments to discuss the news amongst themselves. Then he went on.

'Now as you probably know, Johns manned his expedition entirely with volunteers, whereas we, of course, are all professionals. In addition, we have the advantage of being a smaller group. The lightness of our gear allows us to move more swiftly, and even though we're not kitted out for a long stay at our destination I've no doubt we'll be able to obtain the required facts in good time. Meanwhile, I suggest we follow this river bed as far as we possibly can. Have you taken some bearings, Thorsson?'

'Yes, I have,' came the reply. 'We're still on our correct course.'

'That's good.' Tostig nodded his approval. 'And from now on,' he added, 'we can dispense with leaving helpful markers behind us.'

This produced a round of laughter from the assembled men, who quickly resumed their former activities. The camp comprised five pocket tents, one for each member of the team. There was also a slightly larger tent for storage. All could be folded away at a moment's notice. Tostig was travelling with a total of ten mules, and great care was taken to ensure that their loads were distributed equally. This having been done, Tostig and Thegn led the way forward, with Snaebjorn, Thorsson and Guthrum following close on. It was still early morning.

All five were clad in pea jackets. The party had not yet encountered the sort of harsh weather conditions that were prevalent further west, and for the time being had no need for woollen headgear. Instead they each wore a navy cap with a red band. Tostig's was distinguished by three silver stars, Guthrum's by two, while the others had one star apiece.

'So how are you enjoying our battle with the famous Mr Johns?'

Tostig had addressed his question to Thegn, who was

doing his best to keep pace alongside him.

'Oh, it's a great honour, sir,' he replied. 'I'm in your debt for allowing me to take part.'

'Nonsense,' said Tostig. 'You owe me nothing. You're here on your own merit, the same as everybody else.'

'Well, I'll do my best to help us succeed.'

'If our good fortune continues I'm certain we will.'

Thegn paused and glanced back at the line of mules moving slowly along in their wake. Then he doubled his step and again caught up with his leader.

'Is it true you met Johns a few years ago?' he asked.

'No,' rejoined Tostig. 'We've never spoken.'

'But I thought you both attended the first conference.'

'We did, but to tell you the truth I barely even caught sight of him. From the outset he kept a very low profile and made little or no attempt to "confer" in the true sense of the word. At the time I was quite unaware that the two of us were pursuing similar ideas. An introduction would have been mutually beneficial, but I'm afraid it wasn't to be. As you know, he didn't bother with the second conference.'

'"Time for Action not Words,"' said Thegn.

'Indeed.'

'Blowing his own trumpet, more like.'

'Oh, I didn't begrudge him his blaze of publicity,' said Tostig. 'The world at large needed to know what was proposed. But he seemed to take it as a foregone conclusion that he alone was going to light the way. Which was when I decided to come along and see what could be done. It just happened that we landed before he did.'

'Presumably he'll be aware of our presence?'

'No doubt at all. There's only one navigable approach to that coast, so he must have seen our vessel. Besides, he was bound to make use of the blockhouse.'

'Yes, of course.'

'Johns knows we're here all right.'

Thegn did not pursue the conversation further, as he was now obliged to help encourage the mules to enter a deep cleft where the river banks converged. The visibility was rather poor here, and only after some careful handling by Snaebjorn were they induced into the narrow opening. At this point the sand gave way to sedimentary rock, suggesting that at one time a strong torrent had funnelled through the gap. Tostig watched as the last mule hesitated, pulling back on its rope before finally plunging forth to join the others.

'They'll have to get accustomed to this gloom sooner or later,' he remarked to Guthrum. 'We'll be travelling in near darkness very shortly.'

'How many days' sunlight are there left?' Guthrum enquired.

'Fourteen, according to Thorsson's calculations.'

'And then the real test will begin.'

'Quite.'

Snaebjorn had taken over the leading of the mule train. He cajoled his charges painstakingly along the gorge, avoiding fallen rocks that lay scattered in their path. The river bed soon became sandy again, but it was clear the journey had entered a new phase. In place of crumbling banks there rose on either side steep walls that echoed to every sound.

'So now we are fully committed to our course,' said Tostig. 'Henceforward we need not worry whether the route we have chosen is the correct one or not. The topography of the region has made that decision for us, and we can do nothing about it. Instead we must concentrate all our efforts into moving ahead rapidly and efficiently.'

Each of Tostig's mules had a small bronze bell hung from a collar around the neck. These bells jingled in unison as the little troop wove its way onwards, the march not ceasing until the pervasive dullness had faded into a premature dusk. Then, at last, Tostig gave orders to make camp. Lanterns were lit and the tents erected in a straight row, side by side, at the foot of the rock wall. Meanwhile, Snaebjorn set about preparing supper.

'There'll be no need to tether the mules tonight,' Tostig announced. 'Not in this dismal place. Just turn them loose and they'll keep near us. Now Guthrum and I are going for a short exploratory stroll.'

A little later, Snaebjorn came out of the supply tent and crossed to the cooking area. Then he returned to the tent once more. Emerging a second time, he was met by Thegn.

'Yes?' he said.

'Looking for these?' asked Thegn. He was holding a set of miniature weighing scales.

'As a matter of fact I am,' replied Snaebjorn. 'I've been searching all over the place.'

'My apologies.'

'What are you doing with them?'

'I've been pursuing a line of enquiry,' said Thegn. 'I borrowed them to try something out.'

'I see.'

'You know, it's marvellous the organisation that's gone into this voyage of ours. Quite exhaustive! Every aspect was planned beforehand, right down to the finest detail. For example, how do you think the weight of a water canister compares with a tin of biscuits?'

'No idea,' said Snaebjorn.

'Have a guess.'

'I've just told you I don't know.'

'Identical,' Thegn announced. 'They both weigh exactly the same.'

'Really.'

'Within an ounce. Apparently there were such huge logistical demands to be met that for purposes of simplification all items were classified in fixed units of weight. You could substitute a folded tent, say, with a coiled rope and it would make no difference to the overall load. The exact method used is described in the Ship's Manual, if you're interested.'

'I'll bear it in mind.'

'Appendix B.'

Snaebjorn took the scales and held them up for examination. 'You're very well informed considering you were such a latecomer,' he remarked. 'Everything was stowed by the time you came on board.'

'Couldn't be helped,' Thegn answered. 'I arrived as quickly as I could.'

'That's no excuse for borrowing the scales without permission.'

'Didn't say it was.'

'They're for measuring out portions, not conducting experiments.'

'All right, I'm sorry. It won't happen again.'

There was a movement in the dark and Tostig appeared.

'How's supper going?' he enquired.

'Won't be long,' said Snaebjorn. 'I've broken open the new pouches.'

'The dried food?'

'Yes.'

'Ah, good,' said Tostig. 'Here, Thegn, you should find this most interesting. Come and look.'

They followed Snaebjorn to the cooking area, where a large pot of water was just coming to the boil.

'Dried food is the undoubted miracle of our times,' Tostig continued. 'It provides the key to long-distance travel, and removes the need for all those heavy sacks we used to have to carry. Our supplies are the results of limited research, but even at this preliminary stage we've managed to make huge reductions. In the near future a whole meal will be stored in a cube no bigger than a gaming dice.'

'Sounds invaluable,' said Thegn.

'Certainly it's invaluable,' agreed Tostig. 'And, of course, there are hidden advantages as well. It means we'll be spared from having to dine with people we can't abide. We can simply take our cube and eat alone. What do you say, Snaebjorn?'

'Invaluable,' murmured Snaebjorn, before disappearing into the gloom. Returning with a small linen pouch, he poured the contents into the pot.

'Is that it?' asked Thegn.

'That's it,' said Tostig. 'A meal for five. Better call the others.'

'We're here,' said Guthrum.

* * *

Under normal conditions it took five minutes for a pocket tent to be taken down, folded up and packed away. In twilight the task tended to take a little longer, but nevertheless Tostig insisted that it be practised daily as a precaution in case they ever needed to leave an area quickly. Only Snaebjorn could do it in less than five. The others seldom witnessed this feat because he was always the earliest to rise and he would put his tent away immediately. Their first morning in the gorge found him pacing around as the darkness gradually gave way to a pale dawn light. Having already fed the mules and put the pan on for breakfast, he could now only wait until his companions awoke. He'd found the mules gathered together at the very edge of the camp, a place they'd occupied throughout the long hours of night. During that time the occasional jingling of a bell had indicated one or another of them moving to what it thought was a more comfortable position, before again settling down to rest. Like Snaebjorn, the mules, too, were waiting. After a while he wandered over to the rock wall. Finding a foothold, he climbed a short distance on to a ledge, where he sat for several minutes gazing at the silent row of tents below him. Nothing stirred. No birds. No insects. Nothing. With some difficulty, he got down again and then glanced at the palms of his hands. These now bore a slight blue stain. He was still studying them when Guthrum appeared at the entrance of his tent. Emerging fully clothed, he stood up and put his cap squarely on his head. Then he saw Snaebjorn and gave him a nod.

'How are your two stars suiting you?' Snaebjorn enquired.

'They suit me well enough,' replied Guthrum. 'How does your one star suit you?'

'It's all right.'

'Get any sleep?'

'Four hours.'

'Plenty enough for you.'

'Plenty enough for anyone.'

'Maybe so,' said Guthrum. 'But six hours is what's allowed, so if any of the other men wish to have a "lie-in" they're fully entitled to it.' He gestured towards the cooking area. 'I see you've been busy. What's for breakfast?'

'Same as yesterday.'

'And just as delicious, I hope?'

'Naturally.'

'Morning already?' said Tostig, poking his head out of a second tent. The sound of his voice quickly brought Thegn and Thorsson to their doors too, and within moments everyone had risen.

Straight after breakfast Snaebjorn began preparing the mules for the day's journey, first roping them together in a line, and then loading them up, one by one. He was checking the inventory when Thegn came over and offered to assist. Snaebjorn politely refused, saying it was probably simpler for him to do it himself. Thegn persisted, however, and was finally allowed to help with the 'tying off' of each completed load.

'I suppose you'll need to learn this sooner or later,' Snaebjorn conceded. 'So hold the mule steady and watch while I show you. This section of rope in my left hand is called the standing part.'

'Standing part,' repeated Thegn. 'Right.'

'Now you take the other section, make a loop, pass it round the standing part and twist, like so. Then you pull the loose end through until you have the correct tension, and tie it off. See?'

After a second demonstration Thegn said he thought he'd got the hang of it and attempted to tie a load himself. Snaebjorn said the result was passable but he'd prefer to re-tie it, if Thegn didn't object. When they moved on to the next mule Snaebjorn did the tying off. And again with the one after that. In the meantime, Thegn stood watching in silence. Eventually the last mule was given its load, at which point Tostig wandered over.

'I see you've found yourself a helpmeet,' he remarked.

'I didn't find him,' Snaebjorn answered. 'He found me.'

'I've been learning the ropes,' said Thegn. 'It's been most interesting.'

'I'm glad to hear it.'

'And it reminded me of a question I've been meaning to ask.'

'Which is?'

'Well, I was wondering if these mules have any idea what's in store for them.'

'Of course not,' said Tostig. 'Why should they have?'

'It's just that they seem very quiet.'

'That's a good sign, not a bad one. You don't want excitable mules on a journey like ours.'

'But look how reluctant they were to come into this gorge. If it hadn't been for Snaebjorn's superb handling, we'd practically have had to drag them along. It struck me that they might create problems for us later. When they begin to realise.'

'They won't give us any problems,' said Tostig. 'I've been dealing with mules for a good few years now and I can assure you they have no comprehension beyond the daily round of work, food and rest. They've no inkling whatsoever of our destination. All that business at the beginning of the gorge was merely the shadows making them jumpy. Everyone knows they don't like the dark. Look at them now they've got used to it: they're as placid as anything. Don't worry, Thegn. So long as we don't overburden them, they'll be fine.'

'Oh well, I bow to your better judgment,' Thegn replied. 'I hope you don't mind my raising the subject?'

'Of course not. It's always better to speak out if you have any doubts. Now I'm quite pleased that you and Snaebjorn have managed to team up so effectively because I want the pair of you to lead the way this morning. Guthrum and I checked the ground ahead briefly last night and it looks reasonable, so whenever you're ready.'

'We're ready now,' said Snaebjorn.

'All fed?'

'Yes.'

'All packed?'

'Yes.'

'Excellent,' said Tostig. 'I really don't know what we'd do without you, Snaebjorn.'

A short while later the party moved off, keeping in strict single file. Snaebjorn was at the fore. Carrying a weighty pack on his shoulders, he now took the role of pathfinder, with Thegn and the mule train following close behind. Next came Thorsson, then Tostig and finally Guthrum in the rear. The gorge continued to deepen, and as it did the light became yet more dim. The dry walls towered above them on either side, occasionally letting fall a shower of broken rock flakes, but for the most part appearing quite substantial. From time to time, Thorsson would stop and record their supposed position in his logbook. (The land being untried and therefore uncharted, his conclusions were based mainly on guesswork. Even so, they had enabled him and Tostig to begin work on a basic map whose details they augmented each evening as the expedition progressed.) While Thorsson made his notes, the two men behind him paused to take stock of their situation. Sometimes a brief exchange would ensue if a question arose concerning some difficult terrain, or the timing of the next rest break, but generally each would remain silent with his own thoughts as he waited to resume again, the only sound being the echoed jingling of bells from somewhere ahead. No sooner had Thorsson put his book away than the three of them would be off again, always maintaining single file, and gradually catching up with the mules.

'Did you notice yesterday?' said Tostig. 'When we were looking across at Johns and his companions. Did you notice the very blueness of the scree?'

'Actually I did,' replied Guthrum.

'And you assumed it was a trick of the light?'

'Yes.'

'So did I,' Tostig concurred. 'That was why I didn't

mention it at the time. But now I'm beginning to think it's indigenous to this land we're in. Several times today I've seen the same blueish colour occurring in the rock strata. Most extraordinary.'

It was evening, and the two of them had again embarked on a brief stroll forward of the encampment. Now they stood dwarfed below soaring heights, while night advanced slowly upon them.

'Maybe we could collect a few geological samples on our return journey,' suggested Guthrum.

'Yes, that's what I have in mind,' said Tostig. 'Obviously we must not be distracted from our main purpose by the prospect of undiscovered minerals and so forth. On the other hand, a small rock or two shouldn't add much to our burden.'

'Not if they're packed correctly.'

'We'll get Snaebjorn to do it; he's the expert. Oh, by the way, I happened to overhear your conversation with him this morning. He mentioned the two stars on your cap.'

'He did, yes.'

'Tell me something. Does Snaebjorn have pretensions of leadership?'

'Not as far as I know.'

'Then why the reference?'

'It's simply that he and I go back a long way,' said Guthrum. 'We were engaged in a form of light-hearted rivalry and no more.'

'I see.'

'Snaebjorn meant nothing by it, I assure you.'

'Good.' A few moments passed while Tostig stood

silent amidst the encroaching gloom. Then, in a brighter tone, he turned and spoke again. 'Guthrum,' he said. 'You remain my trusted Number Two.'

'Thank you, sir,' came the reply.

Almost immediately they were hailed by a third voice, coming from some distance behind them. 'I'm afraid I can't see you!'

'Just here!' called Guthrum.

'Ah, thank you!' returned the voice, and a minute later Thegn emerged from the darkness.

'Something wrong?' asked Tostig.

'Oh, no,' said Thegn. 'Sorry if I alarmed you, but all the tents are up, supper's on, and there was nothing left to do; so I took the liberty of wandering along to find the "forward party".'

Guthrum cast a quick glance at Tostig, then proceeded to gaze solemnly at the ground. Meanwhile, a faint smile crossed Tostig's face.

'Well, you've found us,' he said. 'And we're just on our way back.'

'How did the reconnaissance go?' Thegn enquired.

'Very interestingly.'

'Is . . .'

Thegn was forced to break off because without a word his two commanders suddenly stalked off in the direction he'd just come. He followed in their wake, peering now and again at his dim surroundings, but asking no further questions.

When they reached camp they came across Thorsson, hard at work updating the rudimentary map. A large sheet of paper had been unfolded and spread out on the ground, with a lamp placed close by, and Thorsson was kneeling over it. In a case beside him lay a number of pens, each of a different ink, which he was using to add more detail, shading in the latest section of the gorge and writing its estimated dimensions. Also shown were the lower reaches of the dry river bed, the coastal area around the block-house, and the region of scree to their west. The greater part of the map was blank, except for a point in the far corner where a bold X had been marked, along with the letters AFP.

'Ah, Thorsson,' said Tostig. 'Looks as if you'll be on your knees for many hours yet.'

'I don't doubt it,' Thorsson replied.

Just outside the circle of light stood Snaebjorn. He gazed down in silence, regarding Thorsson as he care-fully transferred measurements from his logbook on to the map. Meanwhile, Thegn walked round and crouched down by the far corner.

'Is this the Agreed Furthest Point?' he asked, indi-cating the bold figure X.

'Correct,' said Tostig.

'We've still got a long way to go then.'

'Oh yes,' was the answer. 'An awfully long way.'

They all watched while Thorsson completed the day's observations; then Snaebjorn announced that supper was ready. This was enjoyed by each individual alone in his tent, after which the lamps were extinguished. A stir of bells at the foot of the rock wall signified the spot where the untethered mules had settled down for the night. It was starting to get cold and they'd gathered close together for the long wait until dawn.

Next morning Thegn made a point of being first up, even before Snaebjorn.

'Glad I've caught you,' he said quietly, as the latter emerged from his tent. 'I was wondering if I could give you a hand with the mules today?'

'You can if you want,' Snaebjorn replied.

'In particular I'd like to go over the ropes again, to make sure I've got to grips with that adjustable knot you showed me.'

'I've already given you several demonstrations. Weren't they enough?'

'Unfortunately, no.'

'Well, you'll have to wait until I've taken my tent down.' Snaebjorn glanced at his wristwatch and then began work, reducing his tent to a neatly rolled pack in four and a half minutes.

'Marvellous,' remarked Thegn. He tagged along as Snaebjorn fed the mules, prepared the men's breakfast, and carried out a host of related duties. Only when these were complete was it time to begin loading.

'Now you know this is the standing part, don't you?' enquired Snaebjorn, holding a section of rope in his hand.

'Yes, got that,' said Thegn.

'Right. Now you take the other part, make a loop, pass it round and twist. Then you pull the loose end through and tie it off. Simple.'

By this time other members of the expedition were up and about, and while the two were thus engaged Thorsson happened to pass by on business of his own. After he'd gone Thegn said, 'That's a fascinating map they're drawing, isn't it?'

'Not a bad job at all,' agreed Snaebjorn.

'Thorsson seems confident he's pinpointed our exact position.'

'He's pretty close, yes.'

Thegn stopped what he was doing and glanced at Snaebjorn. 'How do you mean?'

'I mean that I've cross-checked his calculations and found them to be more or less correct.'

'So are you telling me you understand navigation as well?'

'Of course.'

'Marvellous,' Thegn uttered again. 'Navigation, ropemanship, camp cuisine, mastery of the mules. You really are quite a polymath.'

'I don't know about that,' said Snaebjorn. 'As far as I'm concerned these skills are mere prerequisites for the journey we've undertaken. A man would be a fool not to learn them.'

'So he can be first to plant the flag?' asked Thegn.

'If that is his primary aim, yes.'

'Then I'd better start practising.'

'Thegn!' called Guthrum from the middle of the gorge. 'Have you breakfasted?'

'Yes, thank you!'

'Well, don't forget you haven't taken your tent down yet!'

'I'm just helping load the mules!'

'It's all right,' said Snaebjorn. 'I'll finish here. You'd better go and get packed or they'll very likely leave you behind.'

'They wouldn't do that, would they?' queried Thegn.

'They might, but even if they did you needn't worry: we're leaving a clear trail of prints and you'd soon find us.'

In the event, Thegn was not left behind when they got moving again half an hour later. The day's journey had a marked beginning. Dawn had been cloudy, but just at the moment of departure a few rays of sunlight appeared, bathing the upper walls of the gorge in an acute glow. As the travellers peered up from the murky depths, they could clearly see a thin strata of blue rock compressed between the other layers. Then the rays weakened and the gorge was again cast into shadow. By this stage the diffused light had begun hindering progress considerably. Several times during the morning Tostig called a halt to discuss the matter with Guthrum. They were both in agreement that although the use of lamps was preferable, the relative scarcity of fuel made these items a luxury which should be reserved for camp life only. Therefore they had no alternative but to manage by any means they could. Fortunately, the senior members of the team were well practised in adjusting to difficult circumstances, quickly learning to 'cheat' the twilight as they found their way along the gorge: sometimes by squinting through half-closed eyes; sometimes by listening for echoes; and sometimes by adopting the instinctive course chosen by the mules themselves. In the latter case, Snaebjorn would pause and allow the leading mules to pass him by before following them close at hand, carefully observing their step whilst murmuring quiet encouragement in the gloom. The whole party had by now dropped into the natural rhythm of the mules, moving at a pace which was cautious and unhurried, but which continued relentlessly forth. In this manner another two days and nights passed with only minor obstructions impeding their route. On the third such day, however, around about noon and therefore during the least dull period, the column was brought to a full stop. Snaebjorn had gone ahead to reconnoitre and, finding his path barred by an immense angle of rock, had tried moving round to its left. Here a second monolith lay lodged against the first. A fissure at the right-hand side showed where the rock had peeled away from the gorge. It also provided a passage into which Snaebjorn immediately ventured. But again he was pulled up, this time almost striking his head on a fallen block lying flat across the others. Small bells could now be heard approaching. Returning to meet Thegn, Snaebjorn bade him halt the mules while he sought a third way to the extreme left, but there was none suitable. When Tostig arrived with the remainder of the party, it was decided that he and Guthrum would investigate the area beyond the fissure while the others took a break. Thorsson suggested they carried a lamp with them, but Tostig again insisted they worked only with what restricted light there was. Ducking the Lintel Rock, as it came to be known, they entered the fissure, emerging eventually to discover further congeries of toppled giants: great unhewn chunks reclining in all directions and creating a maze of cul-de-sacs, false leads and ill-defined portals. Several times they selected what seemed a possible route forward, only for their path to peter out after a short distance, or else turn back on itself. Then they tried searching further to their right where, for the first time since they'd left the coast, they were confronted by a breeze. It was harsh and chill, pushing and prodding between the collapsed rocks, and bringing with it an unmistakable sound. Somewhere to the east a ponderous mass of water was roaring: plunging, so it seemed, into an immeasurable deep.

3

'YOU ASKED TO SEE me, Mr Johns?'

'Ah, Summerfield, yes. Do come in out of the cold.'

'Thank you.'

It was late evening. Hitherto, Summerfield had only put his head inside Johns' tent, but now he entered fully and closed the flaps behind him. In the dimly lit interior there was little room to spare. A large part of the floor was covered in bedding, already laid out for the night. Other spaces were crammed with equipment and baggage. Johns was sitting at the camp table with his pens and journal before him. The light from a suspended lamp showed that he had removed his woolly helmet. Now Summerfield did the same, before glancing around him.

'Sit on that crate if you like,' said Johns.

'Thank you.'

Summerfield upended a crate of tinned fruit and sat down. At the corner of the table lay a couple of slim textbooks and a folded map. Also a pocket watch. Johns closed his journal and set it to one side; then he gazed thoughtfully at his visitor.

'You're looking very healthy, Summerfield,' he commented. 'This life of ours seems to suit you.'

'Yes, it does rather.'

'Come from a sporting background, don't you?'

'Yes, I do.'

'Always excelled in the hundred yards dash?'

'It has been known, yes.'

'First rate, Summerfield. First rate.'

Johns reached for one of the textbooks and sat for some moments weighing it in his hands. Then he began examining the jacket in detail, turning the book over to look at both the front cover and the back. Meanwhile, the lamp flickered as a gust of wind struck the side of the tent, causing the canvas to beat spasmodically before subsiding once more.

'All the same, Summerfield,' he said at length, 'I really must ask you to slow down a little when we're on the march. This is not to be taken as any sort of reprimand, but it just won't do for you to go sprinting ahead of the rest of the party. We've lost sight of you altogether once or twice over these past few days, and I'm worried you might disappear without trace. You must understand that I need to consider the welfare of the expedition as a whole. It is vital that we act as a coherent group, whatever our individual tendencies. So please can you bear this in mind next time you're in the lead?'

'Of course, Mr Johns,' Summerfield rejoined. 'And I apologise if I've been a cause for concern. It's just that the thought of Tostig pressing further and further ahead of us is almost intolerable.'

'So that's the reason for your impatience, is it?'

'Mostly, yes.'

'Well, to be frank, Summerfield, I'm not the slightest

bit bothered about what Tostig's doing. As I've said many times before, this is not some sort of contest we're taking part in. For want of a better description, it's an International Joint Scientific Enquiry, and it makes no difference who arrives at our destination first, whether it be us, Tostig, or anyone else for that matter. Don't forget Younghusband and Clark would most probably have got there a decade ago if their luck had held. That was a damned unfortunate business, as it turned out; and if they'd succeeded, of course, they could have saved us all the trouble.'

Johns paused and allowed Summerfield to smile at this remark.

'As for the present,' he continued, 'what counts is progress towards our common goal. The sooner the issue is settled one way or another the better.'

At this point the tent was again blasted from without. The ridge pole shook and the lamp swung momentarily, so that its yellow arc rose and fell several times.

'Besides,' Johns ventured, 'who's to say Tostig is pressing ahead of us anyway? For all we know he may have run into all kinds of difficulties. Your own experience will tell you this whole territory is beset by frightful weather conditions. The wind hasn't ceased for days and I can't imagine it being confined merely to our immediate vicinity. Incidentally, did you come across Chase on your way here? I'm expecting his report at any minute.'

'Yes, I saw him about a quarter of an hour ago,' said Summerfield. 'He was at the edge of the camp taking some readings.'

'Very good,' said Johns, clapping his hands together.

'Well, Summerfield, I hope we've put your mind at rest and you'll no longer feel the need to leave us in a trail of dust.'

'Yes, thank you, sir,' Summerfield answered, rising to his feet.

The textbook to which Johns had earlier paid so much attention now lay flat on the table, with its title displayed in bold letters. Summerfield nodded towards it and asked, 'Would it be at all possible to borrow that for a day or two? So I can refresh myself on the main points?'

'By all means,' Johns replied. 'Borrow it for as long as you wish.'

Summerfield thanked Johns again, slipping the book into the inner pocket of his reefer. Then he went outside, braced himself against the wind, and made his way back through the darkness to his own tent. When he got to the flap he paused for a few seconds before finally going in.

Reposed at the far end was Plover. He lay on his side, outstretched with his legs crossed and his head propped on one hand, facing the doorway.

'And how is our esteemed leader?' he enquired.

'Mr Johns is fine,' replied Summerfield. 'Where's Seddon?'

'Seddon has just gone out.'

'Oh.'

'Something to do with the malt drinks, I believe.'

'Yes.'

After his visit to Johns, Summerfield had omitted to replace his woolly helmet. This he now did, pulling it half over his face and leaving it there while he sat down in his own corner. Plover said nothing more, but continued to lie where he was, staring vaguely at the spirit lamp that hissed intermittently nearby. The two of them remained in their respective positions for about twenty minutes, each silent and isolated from the other, until eventually a muffled voice was heard calling from an outlying part of the encampment.

'Hot drink anybody?!' came the cry.

Summerfield was on his feet in an instant, tugging at his helmet and pulling it into place. As he headed through the flaps he glanced round at his neighbour and said, 'Coming then?'

'No, don't think I'll bother,' answered Plover. 'Not if it means putting my boots back on.'

Having attained a higher altitude than Tostig, the western party still enjoyed a brief margin of light around noon each day. There were no shadows on the fields of scree, save those cast by the travellers themselves, and for a short period they could find their way with comparative ease. This was the time when Chase made his most important observations, taking a sighting of the horizon, vague as it was, to ensure they were still going in the correct direction. He also made a note of their achieved mileage. For the rest of the while, however, the men were obliged to stumble through perpetual gloom, their only guide being the wind that blew steadily in their faces, and always from the north.

With little apparent difference between day and night, Johns had decided on strict adherence to a fixed timetable, so that everyone went to bed and got up at an hour appointed by him. This, he explained, was in order to avoid the dangers of lethargy and disorientation. So it was that at seven o'clock next morning, Cook, Sargent and Medleycott were lying awake in their tent, having just been roused by Scagg. Outside, a gale was blowing.

'Should get away with another five minutes,' Sargent murmured. 'Then it's back out into the teeth.'

Cook groaned and hid his head beneath his blanket.

'Bit rough, isn't it?' said Medleycott.

'That's one way of putting it.'

'Quite interesting, though.'

'Interesting?' said Sargent. 'What, you mean being bashed about by the wind all day long?'

'No, no,' said Medleycott. 'I mean the prospect of existing nocturnally for weeks on end. It's going to be quite a challenge: the light isn't due to improve for another month at least.'

'So I heard.'

'We've a dim road ahead of us.'

'My thoughts exactly.'

Suddenly Medleycott sat up and peered through the slit of the tent flaps.

'It's pitch black out there now,' he announced. 'Yet what sights we've beheld since our journey began. Think of them! The leaden moon floating on a shimmering sea! Sunrise and sunset rolled together into one fiery hue! The burnished skies! The majestic beams spreading over the dip of the hill! Don't they make a wonderful spectacle?'

'Can't say I've ever noticed,' replied Sargent.

A short silence followed, during which the three men groped in the dark for their various clothes and belongings. Then Medleycott said, 'By the way, I hope you fellows don't mind my being billeted with you all this time. It was Scagg who arranged it. I expect you're pretty tired of my company by now, aren't you?'

'Course we're not,' said Cook. 'Are we, Sargy?'

'Course not. These your boots?'

'Thank you, yes.'

Medleycott reached over, causing an object to fall from one of his pockets. 'Ah, my souvenir,' he said. 'I forgot I had that.'

'What is it?' asked Cook.

'Just something foolish. One of those blue pebbles we keep seeing. I picked it up when we first came on to the scree.'

'Ten a penny, aren't they?'

'Yes, I know; I ought to throw it away really, but now I've carried it this far I think I'll probably keep it for when we go home.'

'If we go home,' said Sargent.

At these words Medleycott started. 'You can't mean that,' he said. 'Surely not?'

'Surely nothing,' Sargent replied. 'You said yourself it was rough here.'

'Yes, but . . .'

'Mr Medleycott, I'm just pointing out that nothing's for certain. I've been on trips like this before, and I can tell you it does no good to start talking about going home, especially when we're still heading in the oppo-site direction.'

'No, I suppose it doesn't,' answered Medleycott. 'Not when you put it like that.'

'It's a long way to this blessed Agreed Furthest Point.'

'Yes.'

The tent flaps parted and Scagg's bearded face appeared in the opening. 'Discussing geography, are we?'

'Sort of,' said Medleycott.

'Most commendable.'

In his hand Scagg was holding a lamp, which he now used to direct a ray of light into the tent. This showed that both Sargent and Cook had grown beards, while Medleycott remained clean-shaven.

'Glad to see someone's keeping up standards,' Scagg remarked.

The only other lamp in use that morning was hung on a hook above the foldaway kitchen. Here Seddon laboured over his pans as he prepared breakfast. Blanchflower and Firth had risen an hour earlier to give the mules their boiled mash, and the pair were now lost from view at the camp's periphery. When Medleycott, Cook and Sargent entered the illuminated circle, they found Plover and Summerfield sitting in the lee of a rough stone dyke which had been built hurriedly the previous evening. Construction of such works had become the priority on arrival at each new camping place, simply because there was no other protection from the remorseless wind. Earlier versions consisted of little more than low banks behind which the men could shelter if they hunched down. Lately, however, the dykes had gained height and taken on a slightly curved shape. These improvements were instigated by Summerfield, who strove nightly to provide a little additional comfort for his comrades, and whose efforts were subsequently abandoned when the expedition moved on.

This morning he sat behind his most recent creation, stirring sugar into a steaming bowl of porridge. 'Budge up a bit,' said Cook, squatting next to him with a bowl of his own. 'This weather's blinking perishing.'

They were also joined by Sargent.

'There's hardly room for four,' remarked Plover, who had now been pushed to the end of the row. 'Not by a long chalk.'

As if to emphasise the point, he rose to his feet and finished his porridge whilst wandering slowly around the outskirts of the camp. His place behind the dyke was taken immediately by Medleycott. Scagg, meanwhile, stalked amongst the various stacks of supplies and equipment, his eyes fixed as he carried out a series of counts. Then he produced a notebook, wrote down some figures, and put it away again. 'Doesn't that man ever have a day off?' murmured Cook. 'He's been stocktaking continually since we left the blockhouse.'

'He's making sure his calculations are holding true,' said Summerfield. 'Don't forget there are eleven men to clothe and feed; and two dozen mules to look after. It's quite a tall order.'

'But I thought Seddon was supposed to be quartermaster.'

'He is on a day-to-day basis, yes; but it was Scagg who assembled all the stores in the first place, before we even put to sea. I think he feels a duty of responsibility towards Johns.'

'Well, I wish he'd sit down for five minutes and have some porridge,' said Cook. 'It's wearing me out watching him march about like that.'

'Where is Johns anyway?' enquired Sargent. 'And Chase for that matter?'

'They've gone up to the next ridge,' Summerfield replied. 'Apparently the gale is even worse over the other side. Johns is going to make a decision about whether to press on today, or wait here till tomorrow.'

'I suppose he couldn't have decided before we all got out of bed?'

'It seems not.'

The conversation died down as Scagg retraced his steps and crossed into the cooking area. Here he exchanged a few muffled words with Seddon, but the four watchers heard nothing except the wind howling around the edge of their shelter. It tore through the tiny settlement, pummelling the tents with each violent gust, and threatening to carry away anything that was inadequately secured. On occasion these blasts also caused Seddon's lamp to flare up brightly. Thus it was that all of a sudden Plover came into view. They could see him moving slowly along the camp's outer margin, still carrying his porridge bowl and spoon, as he continued his circumambulation.

'If he keeps coming round this regular we'll be able to tell the time by him,' remarked Cook.

Another flicker of the lamplight showed that Plover no longer walked alone. There was a dark shape moving in the gloom beyond him, and this soon resolved itself into a pair of approaching figures. Johns and Chase were back from their survey of the ridge. The instant they appeared, Sargent murmured something inaudible; then he stood up and headed towards the field kitchen, followed closely by Cook. After handing in their dishes, they crossed to their tent and started taking it down. Likewise, Summerfield busied himself by helping Seddon pack away the cooking gear. This left Medleycott sitting in solitude with his back to the dyke. Seemingly lost in thought, he remained where he was for several minutes, gazing silently towards the south while the wind raged all about him. Only when Scagg returned and began issuing a string of commands was Medleycott's reverie broken. A general stir from the direction of the mules indicated that they were now being roped into train for the day's journey. In the meantime, Plover had ceased his aimless stroll and was engaged with the allocation of loads. Quickly, Medleycott got to his feet and went over to join his tent-mates.

'Sorry I didn't come and lend a hand earlier,' he said. 'I thought we were supposed to be waiting for Johns' decision.'

'We were,' replied Sargent. 'But it was obvious the moment he came back he'd already made his mind up.'

'Why was it obvious?'

'Because he looked so blinking cheerful, that's why!'

Shortly afterwards, everyone was called into the middle of the camp so that Johns could address them. He was wearing a heavy surcoat, as well as his woolly helmet and mittens, and stood braced against the wind.

'Good morning, men,' he said, raising his voice. 'I'm glad to see you're all so keen to press on. In fact, I find it most heartening. Now you might have guessed it's blowing seven bells beyond the ridge, but I've come to the conclusion we would gain nothing by waiting here on the off-chance that it subsides. We'd simply lose another day. So, assuming you've all breakfasted, I'd like to push forward at once, if that's agreeable to everybody?'

'Quite agreeable,' replied Scagg.

'Excellent,' said Johns. 'And by the way, I suggest you don the warmest clothing you have. It's really quite bitter up there.'

At these words he glanced briefly at Plover who, unlike the other men, was still wearing his high-peaked cap. By some fortune this item had stayed on its owner's head during even the worst bouts of wind experienced in the past few days, and had lately become a frequent subject of discussion between Johns and Scagg. On several occasions Johns expressed his opinion that woolly helmets were markedly more suitable for the present conditions than any sort of cap, being both warmer and likelier to stay in place. He urged Scagg to press the point on Plover, but for some reason Scagg persistently failed to do this. Johns never raised the matter directly with Plover himself because, as he told Scagg, it might cause embarrassment. Hence Plover continued to be at odds with his companions: them in their woolly helmets; him in his high-peaked cap.

He was wearing it thirty minutes later when they departed from the camp, leaving Summerfield's stone dyke as the only evidence they had ever been there. No one witnessed whether or not Plover struggled to retain his headgear as they mounted the ridge. Dawn was still some hours away, and the combination of darkness and rising gales meant all their faculties were directed towards finding a passage over the ridge and into the territory beyond. Summerfield pioneered the way, his body bent to the ground; his pace slow but resolute. Then came

Blanchflower and Firth leading the mules, followed by Scagg and the rest of the men in steady procession, with Johns at the rear. The formation had been as such for almost a week now, and at Scagg's suggestion had remained unaltered.

'There won't be any stragglers when they know you're behind them,' he observed to Johns one evening in the seclusion of their tent. 'I'll pull them and you can push them, so to speak.'

'Are you sure that's really necessary?' Johns enquired. 'After all, they're each of them hand-picked volunteers who shouldn't need any inducement.'

'Mark my words, Mr Johns,' replied Scagg. 'Even the keenest volunteer needs the occasional prod in the right direction.'

'Well, all right, if you say so,' said Johns. 'You certainly seem to have the measure of the men.'

A second consequence of this policy was that Summerfield had become de facto leader of the expedition. His enthusiasm apparently undampened by Johns's cautionary words, it was always he who chose where they camped overnight, since he invariably arrived first. During the days of the gales he demonstrated an acute ability in judging the ideal times to rest, pause, or come to a full halt. Often the tail-enders entered a new site to find a rudimentary dyke already under construction, with the suggested position for the field kitchen carefully marked out. At other times Summerfield would get the stove set up temporarily, so that a hot malt drink awaited his comrades when they caught up. Johns seemed content to allow him to continue in the role of trailblazer (so long as he didn't get too far ahead) and remarked to Scagg that this freed them to concentrate on logistical matters. For some while they had been holding regular consultations on the state of their supplies; these being based on Scagg's figures. Regard was also given to the distance covered so far, and the estimated journey ahead. Accordingly, at the end of the twelfth day's march across the scree, Johns and Scagg were occupied in their tent, heads together over a page of calculations.

'Yes, I quite agree,' Johns concluded at length. 'Tomorrow would seem to be most opportune. And you think he can do it on his own?'

'I've no doubt at all,' said Scagg. 'He's a very capable man when he applies himself.'

'Very well. Could you ask him to come and see me?'

'Beg your pardon, but I've already taken the liberty. This should be him on his way now.'

There was a crunching of heavy boots outside the tent, followed by a polite cough, after which Cook's head appeared in the opening. 'You wanted to see me, Mr Johns, sir?'

'Yes, Cook. Step inside, will you?'

Cook did as he was instructed, removing his woolly helmet and clutching it in one hand behind his back. Meanwhile, Scagg stood up and went out. Johns ran his eye over the calculations once more, then glanced at the man before him.

'Fancy a change, Cook?' he said.

'I don't mind, sir.'

'Well, there's a task I'd like you to do for me.'

'Sir.'

'I want you to act as a relay.'

'Sir?'

'Take four mules and make your way back to the block-house.'

'Oh, right, sir.'

'Have a rest for a day or two; then, when you judge the conditions are correct, bring out all the remaining supplies. Come only as far as Summerfield's Depression. With luck we'll meet you there on our return journey. Is that clear?'

'Yes, sir.'

'Good,' said Johns. 'You can leave first thing tomorrow. See Seddon for some rations and any equipment you think you may need. Now, at present you share a tent with Medleycott and Sargent, don't you?'

'I do, sir, yes.'

'All right, well, I think I'll pay them a visit and explain what's happening. Lead on, will you, Cook?'

A few moments later they emerged into the night, where the only illumination came in the form of a weak glow emanating from each of the other three tents. The rest of the camp lay hidden from view as the tireless wind swept over it. Carefully avoiding an array of guy ropes, Cook led the way to his own tent and parted the flaps.

'After you, Mr Johns,' he announced in a loud voice.

Inside, the lamp revealed Medleycott and Sargent reclining against their kit bags. Both peered casually towards the doorway before sitting up sharply to clear a space for their unexpected guest. 'No need for ceremony,' said Johns, ducking inside. With a gleeful look on his face, Cook slipped in behind him. After exchanging a few pleasantries with his men, Johns made some general enquiries into their well-being. He listened earnestly to their replies, then told them about Cook's imminent departure. 'This marks the beginning of the second stage of our operation,' he expanded. 'It has all been worked out by Scagg and myself, and means we should be fully supplied for our return journey. The other side of the coin is that we'll be going on with four less mules than before, so I'm afraid we'll be obliged to jettison some of our gear. We'll be abandoning one of the tents when we leave here tomorrow, as well as select other items, and these measures should help reduce our overall burden. The large telescope, for example, has proved superfluous to requirements, so it can stay behind. Personally I'll be sacrificing my camp table, which I've come to regard as an unnecessary luxury. If any of you wish to make similar gestures they will be greatly appreciated.'

'We will try to give it some thought,' offered Medleycott, at the end of an expectant silence.

'Excellent,' said Johns. 'Well, I'll bid you all good night now, and I apologise for disturbing your evening. Do make sure you get plenty of rest, Cook.'

'I will, thank you, sir. Good night.'

Johns went on to make similar calls at the other tents, imparting the news to their respective occupants. Then he returned to join Scagg, who was again studying his book of figures by lamplight.

'I thought Cook took it rather well,' Johns remarked. 'There he was, faced with countless days of isolation, yet he didn't raise a murmur. Quite admirable really.'

'I expect he'll turn it to his advantage,' said Scagg. 'Cook usually does.'

'By the way, have you had a chance to go over the new sleeping arrangements?'

'I'm just looking at them now, sir. If it's all right with you, I think I'll put Seddon in with Chase, Blanchflower and Firth; then Plover and Summerfield can join Medleycott and Sargent.'

'Four to a tent,' said Johns. 'It's going to be a tight squeeze for them all, isn't it?'

'Fairly tight, yes.'

'Well, maybe we should consider letting one of them share with us?'

'I'm sorry, Mr Johns, but I just won't hear of it,' Scagg replied. 'You need your privacy much more than they do.'

Next morning Cook made the most of his breakfast, returning to Seddon for second and then third helpings. These he was allowed, along with some substantial rations. Sitting on his pack in the lee of the stone dyke, Cook then held forth about the hazards of his impending journey. 'I'll be friendless and all alone,' he whined. 'Lost in the wilderness without even a guiding star.'

'Oh, give it a rest,' said Sargent. 'All you've got to do is follow the trail we came up.'

'I might have known you'd be sympathetic,' replied Cook.

'Here,' said Medleycott, passing him a bar of choco-late. 'Take a piece of this; it'll help sustain you during your odyssey.'

Cook thanked him and prepared to leave. Standing up, he cast his eyes around the encampment. 'Nice here, isn't it?' he remarked. 'I'll really miss this place. Marvellous scenery.'

By now Johns and Scagg had come over and joined the main group.

'Good luck then, Cook,' said Johns, proffering his hand. 'And we'll see you at Summerfield's Depression.'

'Thank you, sir,' Cook replied, before turning to the assembled men. 'Well, everybody, I'll be thinking of you with envy when I get back to the blockhouse. You'll be enjoying the luxury of your utility blankets, while I'll have to put up with sheets, pillows and a mattress.'

'All right, Cook, that'll do,' murmured Scagg. 'Now get a move on or we'll send someone else.'

Cook saluted, snatched up his pack and with a hearty farewell disappeared in the direction of the mules. A few moments later he could be heard detaching the four he had chosen for the journey; then he was gone. After breakfast the camp was dismantled. At the same time a depot was established, consisting of the surplus tent and numerous other items deemed no longer necessary. A small cache of emergency provisions was also left at this point. Johns expressed himself well pleased with the resulting 'lightweight' expedition that prepared to leave an hour later. In addition, he read out the names of the men who would occupy each remaining tent. Plover appeared to have some difficulty absorbing this announcement, and asked for the list to be repeated. Once he'd heard it again he lapsed into silence.

Just prior to departure, Scagg was approached by Blanchflower and Firth, who spoke to him with some urgency. He in turn asked for a discreet word with Johns.

'What is it, Scagg?' Johns enquired, when they'd moved away from the other men.

'Cook has taken four females,' Scagg replied. 'Blanchflower and Firth noticed when they were loading up. He should have used two of each gender, shouldn't he?'

'Of course he should,' said Johns. 'One would have thought that was obvious to anybody.'

'I suppose no one explained it to him?'

'Well, I certainly didn't.'

'Neither did I.'

'How irksome! It means we'll have fewer mating pairs available.'

'Shall I send Sargent after him?'

Johns sighed and slowly shook his head. 'No, Scagg, he'll be too far away by now. We can't afford to lose any more time, not with the supplies beginning to dwindle. It will just have to be another case of managing with the mules we have. And I suppose we can hardly blame Cook if we didn't spell it out syllable by syllable.'

There was a short pause as Scagg cleared his throat. This caused Johns to glance at him quickly. 'Is there something else?'

'I'm afraid I've blundered too, sir,' Scagg answered. Reaching into his pocket he produced a key, which he allowed to rest in the palm of his hand. 'I forgot to hang this on the hook when we left the blockhouse. The door's locked.'

'Dear oh dear, Scagg,' said Johns. 'That's very unlike you.'

'I know, sir, and I really must apologise. I can only think my mind was otherwise engaged. Fortunately, the reserve supplies were all stacked outside, so they'll be quite accessible to Cook.'

'Fortunate indeed.'

'But he'll miss out on his sheets, pillows and mattress.'

'Well, well,' uttered Johns. 'Maybe he'll learn not to be so damned clever in future. I presume he's still got his utility blanket?'

'Yes, and a spare one as well, I think.'

'All right then. He'll simply have to wrap up warm at night, won't he?'

Their meeting concluded, the pair turned and rejoined the rest of the party.

'How's the wind, Chase?' Johns asked.

'Dead ahead, sir,' came the answer. 'No change since yesterday.'

'Looks as if there's another hard march in store for us. Can you tell Summerfield we're ready to proceed?'

'Very well, sir.'

'Oh, and Chase,' Johns added. 'When you come to mark this place on the map, put it down as Cook's Folly, will you?'

'As you wish.'

Johns waited while Chase went forward and passed the word to Summerfield. Then, after another minute, the mule train began moving. Slowly it advanced into the darkness, with Blanchflower and Firth at its head, while the rest of the men fell in behind. Eventually only Plover and Johns were left.

'Everything all right, Plover?' Johns asked, when Plover failed to stir.

'Yes, quite all right, thank you,' Plover replied.

'And you're enjoying our little jaunt, I hope?'

'So far, yes.'

'Good. Good.' Johns waited a little longer, and then said, 'Well, off you go then, Plover, or we'll both be left behind.'

'Of course, Mr Johns, so sorry,' said Plover, turning abruptly and setting off in pursuit. Johns watched him for a few moments before following in his tracks.

The way they went was over yet another ridge in the apparently endless scree. For twelve consecutive days the party had toiled up, then down, then always up again. This morning, however, as dawn gradually drew near, a change seemed to be imminent. After they'd mounted a second ridge they found that subsequently the gradient continued to decline, with no indication of any further rise. The gale still blasted them without mercy, but nonetheless by the time they stopped for a break a mood of optimism was abroad. Sitting in the subdued light of noon, their backs to the wind, Johns and Scagg discussed the prospects for success.

'I'm confident that this scree will continue to run downhill from now on,' Johns surmised. 'Then we can look forward to it levelling out into a plain.'

'Our rate of progress has started to improve already,' said Scagg.

'Yes, indeed it has,' said Johns. 'And with it the men's spirits. The only exception is Plover. I'm rather concerned; we've hardly heard a peep from him all morning. Why do you think that is, Scagg?'

'He probably doesn't like being squashed in a tent with three others.'

'Can't be helped on a journey like this. It's all for one and one for all.'

'I don't think Plover sees it like that, Mr Johns.'

'You mean he's a snob?'

'I wouldn't like to say, sir.'

'So he is a snob then. Well, I must admit I've noticed he isn't much of a mixer. Never seems to want to join in with the spirit of things. And he still insists on wearing that high-peaked cap of his all the time. By the way, did you get the chance to have a word with him about that?'

'Not yet, no. Sorry.'

'Because the last thing we need is Plover frozen stiff on account of . . .'

Johns broke off as Plover suddenly appeared to their left, carrying a steaming mug in his hand. When he saw them looking at him he paused and nodded, but did not approach.

'Ah, hot drinks,' said Johns, rising to his feet. With a nod towards Plover, he strode off in the direction of the field kitchen. Scagg, meanwhile, stood up and straightened his surcoat. Then he wandered over to Plover.

'Expect your ears are smarting, aren't they?' he said.

'Not particularly,' Plover replied. 'Are yours?'

'No, they're not,' said Scagg. 'But I'm surprised yours aren't. Very surprised.'

After Scagg had left him, Plover remained where he was for several minutes. He gazed into the distance whilst finishing his drink, then returned his empty mug to Seddon. Next he located his pack and unfastened the straps. Delving inside, he found a woolly helmet, which he immediately substituted for his high-peaked cap.

'Sorry I can't offer anyone a piece of chocolate,' said Medleycott. 'I'm afraid Cook walked off with the whole bar.'

'Actually I think I've got some hidden somewhere,' answered Summerfield. 'I'll have a look for it later.'

It was the evening of the same day, and bedding was being laid out for the night. The three tents had been erected in a kind of half-circle, their entrances adjacent to one another, with Johns's tent at the centre, facing due south. His neighbours to the east were Medleycott, Summerfield, Sargent and Plover, though for the moment Plover was absent.

'He said he was going for a look around outside,' Medleycott informed his companions.

'Well I hope he comes back soon,' said Sargent. 'I want to get some sleep.'

'Why don't you take the berth at the far end?' suggested Summerfield. 'Then you won't be disturbed by anyone.'

'Because I like being by the door,' Sargent replied.

'I'll take it then, if nobody minds.'

At that instant the canvas parted and Plover came in. Rather than closing the flaps quickly behind him, however, he paused in the opening to remove his boots, so that a rush of cold air flooded into the tent. As the lamp flickered, Medleycott and Sargent glanced at each other but said nothing. Plover, in his turn, spoke to nobody. Meanwhile, Summerfield stretched out on his utility blanket. He was still wearing his reefer jacket, and after a few seconds he sat up again. Reaching into his inside pocket, he produced the textbook Johns had lent him some days earlier. It had a plain grey cover with bold black lettering:

The Theory of Transportation
by
F. E. Childish

Holding the book towards the lamplight, Summerfield began reading.

4

'THEGN, I'M LOOKING FOR a volunteer,' said Tostig. 'I need someone to take a line and try and find a way across this maelstrom. It won't be easy; the task requires both daring and judgment; one slip could mean certain death. I thought I'd give you first refusal.'

'Thank you, sir.'

'Obviously, Snaebjorn would do it at the drop of a hat, but the truth is he's far too valuable to the expedition. We simply couldn't afford to risk losing him, so if I could send you instead it would be a great help.'

'Well, yes, I'd definitely like to have a go at it, if you think I'm capable.'

They were standing at the edge of a deep chasm. Below them poured the huge volume of water they had heard as they approached. Strewn with immense boulders, it seethed and roared before tumbling over precipitous falls into a vast unseen cauldron.

'What calamity could have struck this land?!' demanded Tostig. 'What violent upheaval to drive a river completely off its course?! It is unbelievable! Never have I known such geological chaos. I brought you here so you could witness it for yourself prior to making a decision.'

'That's much appreciated.'

They stepped back as the rocky shelf they stood on was dashed with flying spray.

Then Tostig continued.

'To put it bluntly, Thegn, this could spell disaster for us. It has actually placed us in a worse boat than Johns. Oh, I know it must be hard-going on that scree, but at least he has an open road ahead of him. Our path, by contrast, is beset with pitfalls of every kind. If we can't find a way forward we'll be beaten, and our mission will fail. I presume you wouldn't want that to happen?'

'No, of course not,' said Thegn.

'Then our next move depends on you.'

Another dash of spray rose up and fell again. Treading carefully, Thegn went to the edge of the rocks and looked down at the furious torrent.

'I suppose it would require a light line,' he offered at length.

'A lifeline?' said Tostig. 'What do you mean by that?'

'No, no, a light line,' Thegn repeated. 'So that I can venture further. I could use it to pull a heavier rope across. People who build bridges employ a similar method, so I believe. Once the first rope is anchored, it's quite easy to add a second, then a third, and so on.'

'Thegn, I don't want a bridge,' said Tostig. 'I simply want you on the other side of this river. Guthrum is in charge of all ropes, so if you've got a preference you'd better speak to him about it. Now have you seen enough?'

'Yes, I think so.'

'Well, let's get into some shelter. Come on.'

Tostig turned and led the way back towards the Lintel

Rock, where their companions were tending to the mules. After a consultation with Guthrum, it was decided that Thegn's crossing would be attempted the following noon, and in the meantime they would make camp.

'Here is a fine opportunity to replenish our water supplies,' announced Tostig. 'In fact, it might be our last chance for quite a while. Can you see to it, Snaebjorn?'

'I'll begin right away.'

'Let me help,' said Thegn, rising to his feet.

'No, you take a rest,' Tostig countered. 'Thorsson can assist Snaebjorn. You'll need all your strength for tomorrow's ordeal. And incidentally, if you have any valuables in your possession I suggest you leave them with Guthrum or myself for safekeeping.'

'I brought nothing of any worth,' said Thegn. 'Before we embarked I received instructions to travel as lightly as possible, so naturally I complied.'

'Then at least give me the star from your cap,' said Tostig. 'Without it there'll be naught to remind us of the glory of your quest.'

'Unless I succeed.'

'If you succeed you will be granted due recognition; possibly even a mention on the map.' Tostig held out his hand to receive Thegn's silver star, which he then dropped into a side-pocket. 'Now I suggest you go to bed early. Find a place amongst these rocks to pitch your tent, and we'll see you in the morning.'

After Thegn had retired, Tostig and Guthrum spent some time examining Thorsson's map, which they'd laid out on top of a large flat boulder. Much detail had been added in the past few days, although it was still far from complete. By lamplight they studied the latest additions: namely, the Lintel Rock and the rapids beyond. Thorsson had made extensive use of the light-blue pen to mark the course of the dry river bed, with a darker hue for the river itself.

'It's getting to be quite a tour de force,' remarked Guthrum.

'Without doubt,' concurred Tostig. 'Thorsson has done a very thorough job. Yet there's one thing that worries me about this map of ours. I'm concerned that the finished version could become a cause of mistrust between ourselves and our comrades. After all, whoever controls the map controls the route.'

'Indeed.'

'Therefore, I propose that when we reach our destination the map should be divided into separate sections, one for each man. This could be four or five, depending on the outcome of Thegn's jaunt tomorrow. I think you'll agree that it will probably be better not to mention the matter to Thorsson for the time being. He may lose heart if he discovers his masterpiece is going to be cut up. Then there's the question of Thegn himself . . .'

As he spoke, Tostig casually reached into the pocket containing Thegn's silver star. 'Hello, what's this?' he said, pulling out a folded sheet of notepaper. Holding it to the lamp, he peered at it closely before uttering a surprised, 'Well, well, well.'

'What is it?' asked Guthrum.

'See for yourself,' Tostig answered, handing it over. 'I thought all my correspondence had been filed away when we sailed, but this must have somehow slipped through the net.'

Guthrum took the note and read:

My dear Tostig
I have just received your message and now hasten to reply. Yes,
by all means feel free to make full use of the blockhouse. Clark
and I built it for the very purpose of providing a staging post
for those who arrive at that desolate shore. Needless to say, I
am delighted you've decided to give Commander Johns a run
for his money. Maybe at last this issue can be settled once and
for all. I wish both parties good luck in their endeavours.
  Yours sincerely
    R. F. Younghusband

'Written in his own hand,' observed Guthrum, returning the note. 'You were highly honoured.'

'A courteous rejoinder to a polite enquiry,' said Tostig. 'Just as one would expect from the great man.'

'An adventurer of the old school.'

'Unquestionably.'

'Why did he and Clark turn back? I never quite understood the reason.'

'You might well ask. The official explanation was given as "navigational difficulties", but the truth was that they lost all their mules whilst still at sea. Apparently the wretched creatures succumbed to a form of melancholia during a storm: you know how easily they can become dispirited. One by one they died and had to be thrown overboard. A very trying episode, as you might imagine. Nevertheless, the voyagers pressed on and eventually made land. By building the blockhouse Younghusband and Clark greatly improved the chances of their successors, but in terms of their own plans the expedition was a disaster. They never got beyond the beachhead. Naturally, the cause of the failure was suppressed as long as possible for fear of undermining the Theory.'

'Naturally.'

'And I'm afraid the story has a sad postscript: poor Clark died on the homeward journey. I gather he was buried at sea.'

In silence, Tostig and Guthrum resumed their perusal of the map. For several minutes neither spoke, and the only sound was the distant roar of the river. Then, at last, approaching footsteps indicated the return of Snaebjorn and Thorsson from their duties at the water's edge. After reporting that all the canisters were now fully replenished, Snaebjorn went off with Guthrum to feed the mules and erect the remaining tents. In the meantime, Tostig took Thorsson to one side.

'I'd like a quiet word, if you don't mind,' he murmured. 'While our colleagues are otherwise engaged.'

'Nothing wrong, I hope?' said Thorsson. 'Surely not a mistake with the map?'

'No, no, of course not,' replied Tostig. 'I merely wish to sound you out in a general way, that's all. You are no doubt aware that Thegn is planning to assay the rapids tomorrow?'

'I guessed as much.'

'Well, I was wondering if there was anything you wanted to tell me before he sallies forth? Any salient fact or omission, for example, which you feel I've overlooked and should be brought to my attention; any rumour circulating without my knowledge; any weakness in the chain of command?'

'None that I can think of.'

'And you'll agree that in our current circumstances each member of the party is dependent on everyone else?'

'Indeed.'

'Then tell me, Thorsson, would you invest Thegn with your life at the end of a rope?'

'Yes, I would.'

'Equally Snaebjorn?'

'Without hesitation.'

'And they you?'

'I should certainly like to think so.'

'Excellent. Quite excellent.' Tostig returned to the map and gave it a final inspection before rolling it up for the evening. Then he looked across at his navigator. 'Thorsson,' he said. 'You remain my trusted Number Three.'

'Thank you, sir,' came the reply.

The following day around about noon, four men watched as a coil of rope gradually unwound. One end was anchored to a pillar of rock overlooking the river; the other had been tied round Thegn's waist before he disappeared into the gloom.

'Now we can only wait,' said Tostig.

His voice was all but drowned out by the continuous din that rose up from the waters below. Thegn had chosen to begin the crossing by descending a flight of natural steps he'd discovered a short distance upriver from the camp. Leaving his belongings with Snaebjorn, he'd asked them all to wish him luck before carefully starting down. Hereafter the only indication of his progress would be the slowly moving rope that slithered over the rocks and into nothingness.

Little by little the coil diminished, sometimes in a steady flow, sometimes in a series of fitful jerks interspersed with long halts. Thegn was clearly being very cautious. Presently the rope went slack along its entire length, as if he was coming back towards them. Everyone waited; a minute passed, then another, but still the rope remained slack.

'Shall I take some in?' suggested Guthrum.

'Good idea,' Tostig replied.

Guthrum stepped forward to seize the rope, but at the same instant it tautened and was off once more, uncoiling wildly as it coursed over the rocks, all the time pulling to the right. While this was happening they heard no cry from Thegn: only the ceaseless roar of the rapids. Within moments the rope had reached its full extent, coming to an abrupt halt and straining hard at its anchor. Immediately, Tostig gave the order for a second line to be added to the first. It was paid out steadily, and by degrees the tension lessened until at last the rope lay freely across the void. Then, after a further period of waiting, they received two sharp tugs from the other end.

'That was the agreed signal,' announced Tostig. 'He has made it safely.'

To celebrate, he asked Thorsson to return to the Lintel Rock and fetch a flask of spirits from the supply tent. Also four little cups. A few minutes later they stood above the torrent and toasted the triumphs of the voyage so far. Then Snaebjorn asked if he could speak to Tostig in private.

'It may be of minor importance,' he said. 'But there's something I think you ought to know.'

Alone at the far side of the river, Thegn secured his line and sat down to rest. He had succeeded only by accident, having lost his footing whilst perched on a boulder halfway across. From there he'd been swept along by the current before suddenly pulling up short when the rope ran out. He had then remained suspended in midstream for a full minute until being released again, eventually casting up battered and bruised on a stony shoal. Only good fortune had prevented him from plunging over the falls, and only after a further struggle had he managed to reach the opposite bank. Now he sat at the top of a low cliff, wet through and temporarily isolated from his comrades. A weak attempt to call in their direction brought no reply, and he in turn heard nothing from them. After a while, however, there came three tugs on the line. Standing up, he repeated the two tugs he had given earlier. The three tugs came again and at once he began hauling, bringing in first his own original line, then the extra length that had been added to it. Finally he drew towards him a much thicker, heavier rope. This he fastened to a rock before signalling with another two tugs. The rope was then pulled tight from the other end, so that it hung like a bridge across the river. The sight of it caused a thin smile to cross Thegn's lips. After another brief rest he began making his way back to where he'd started, hand over hand along the rope, his feet dangling above the churning waters. The return journey took a minute or so. When at last he came in view of the other four men, they were gathered together in a group examining some object which, on seeing him, they immediately hid away. He swung the final few yards towards them and dropped to the ground.

'Ah, Thegn,' said Tostig. 'You're just in time to help us with the mules. It's going to be a long job conveying them all to the opposite side so we'd better get started directly.' He glanced into the chasm. 'I suppose it's a blessing that the visibility is so poor; otherwise they would be certain to panic. Now is this rope quite secure at the other end?'

Thegn assured him that it was, and then Thorsson was asked to bring up the first mule from the camp at Lintel Rock. Meanwhile, Thegn was sent back along the ropeway with a secondary line. The moment Thorsson arrived with the mule, Snaebjorn seized it by one ear and forced it to the ground. Quickly it was trussed up and rendered immobile, then slung under the rope and hauled across the river. Guthrum had joined Thegn on the far bank and was charged with leading each mule away. The process of moving them one by one was necessarily slow, but after a couple of hours the men had succeeded in getting all ten mules transferred. Next came the packs containing the food supplies, followed by the tents and the rest of the equipment. The last items to be brought over were the recently filled water canisters. By now Thegn had made the crossing several times in order to assist the operation at both ends, and was at present working alone with Snaebjorn on the southern bank. As the canisters were dispatched, he commented that it would really have made more sense to replenish them on the new side of the river, rather than the old.

'As if it's any of your business,' said Snaebjorn.

'What do you mean?' asked Thegn.

'Simply that you have a marked tendency to pry. A trait that has not passed unnoticed.'

'By whom?'

'You'll find out soon enough.'

Without another word, Snaebjorn took to the ropeway and began making his way along it. Thegn followed close behind. When they reached the opposite bank, Tostig, Guthrum and Thorsson were waiting for them. The majority of equipment had been moved further inland so that a new camp could be established. Nearby, however, there still remained three packing cases. These had been placed side by side in a row, and a lamp hung from a pole above them.

'Is that everything now?' enquired Tostig.

'Yes,' replied Snaebjorn. 'I've checked the whole site and it's quite clear.'

'Very good, Snaebjorn. You've done a first-class piece of work. Maybe you could begin preparing supper?'

'Right you are.'

As Snaebjorn turned and headed for the shadows, Thegn made to follow him.

'Just a moment, Thegn,' said Tostig.

'Sir?'

'Come and stand before me, please.'

Thegn complied.

'Is something the matter?' he asked.

'We have yet to discover.' Tostig paused and regarded Thegn for a long moment before continuing. 'Thegn, it has been brought to my notice that you keep amongst your belongings a copy of the Ship's Manual.'

'Ah,' replied Thegn.

'A brief search has confirmed the fact.'

'Yes. It would.'

'Are you not aware that this contravenes regulations; that you may have put the ship and its company in peril; and that therefore you have placed yourself under suspicion of conspiracy?'

'No, I'm sorry, I didn't know.'

'Ignorance of the regulations is no excuse,' said Tostig. 'I'm afraid your case will have to be heard by a tribunal. This will be convened at once. Your judges will be Guthrum, Thorsson and myself.'

At a given signal, the three senior figures moved into the circle of light and sat down on the packing cases, the lamp shining above their heads. Then Tostig declared that the tribunal was in session.

'Incidentally,' he added. 'You may wish to know that it was Snaebjorn who denounced you.'

'Yes,' said Thegn. 'I guessed it might have been.'

After a short consultation with his colleagues, Tostig produced the manual from his pocket and held it before him.

'Firstly,' he began. 'How did you come to lay your hands on this?'

'I borrowed it,' Thegn answered.

'Without seeking permission?'

'I didn't think I needed permission.'

'Why not?'

'Well, because . . .' Thegn hesitated. 'Because it belongs to my uncle.'

'And it didn't occur to you that your "uncle" might object?'

'No, it didn't.'

'Or that it could have fallen into the wrong hands?'

'But there's nobody here except us.'

'That makes no difference,' said Tostig. 'The ship is our only lifeline back to civilisation; consequently, the manual must stay with the ship. To bring it inland suggests an ulterior motive. Were you planning, for example, to take command of the vessel on our return journey, so that you could claim credit for the success of the expedition?'

'Of course not.'

'Can you prove that you weren't?'

'No.'

'Were you working under instruction from another agency?'

'Again no.'

'Not Johns?'

'Certainly not Johns.'

'Then who?'

'Nobody.'

'So why did you borrow the manual?'

'It's only a copy.'

'Nevertheless . . .'

'Dammit, I was just trying to show some interest!' cried

Thegn suddenly, his eyes ablaze. 'I merely wanted to further my knowledge of this marvellous enterprise we're involved in! To study it in every aspect; to understand it in all its detail; and to be there when we plant the flag at our destination! The Agreed Furthest Point! Even the name of it spells adventure! No one has ever been there before and it's the opportunity of a lifetime! I know I wasn't your first choice, but I've done all I can to be a useful member of the team! I've hardly slept for weeks and today I risked my neck finding a way across the river! Yet despite my good deeds, my hard work and my attention to duty, I find myself accused of conspiracy! I tell you it's simply not fair!'

In the moments that followed Thegn's outburst, the only sound came from the relentless waters cascading below. All else was quiet. During the past hour the night had deepened, intensifying the glow of the lamplight against the surrounding gloom. The three members of the tribunal said nothing, but sat gazing into the darkness with their arms folded. Thegn, meanwhile, remained standing where he was, and glared balefully at his inquisitors. Not until another minute had elapsed did Tostig break the silence.

'Nothing is fair in this world,' he said.

Just then the remote clanging of a spoon against a pan indicated that supper was almost ready. Accordingly, Tostig announced that the tribunal would be adjourned until further notice. Nobody spoke as the lamp was dimmed and they made their way towards the camp. Here they found that the supply tent had already been erected, as had Thegn's pocket tent.

'I thought I'd save you the trouble,' said Snaebjorn.

'Thank you,' Thegn replied.

'It's in a pleasant, sheltered spot.'

'Yes, so I see.'

Tostig, Guthrum and Thorsson had sat down on some rocks near the cooking area, and they now invited Thegn to join them. A short while later supper was served, direct from the pan.

'You know, it's really quite extraordinary,' said Tostig, adopting a genial tone. 'Every night we have the same meal produced from the same stock of dried food, yet thanks to Snaebjorn it always tastes that little bit different.'

'He has the chef's special touch,' observed Guthrum.

'Quite so.'

'Achieved with the tiniest amount of pepper, maybe, or possibly salt.'

'Yes.'

There followed a period of silence, then Thorsson said, 'By the way, I'll soon need to open another bottle of blue ink.'

'To mark the river?' Tostig enquired.

'Yes,' said Thorsson. 'It's coming to occupy a fairly large area of the map.'

'Well, it can't be helped. That river is a most important detail.'

'Unfortunately, I've had no use for the green ink as yet.'

'No, you won't have.'

'It's a shade that's unknown hereabouts.'

'Indeed.'

During the course of these exchanges Thegn had been sitting quietly amongst his companions, with Thorsson on the one side, and Guthrum on the other. As usual, the meal had consisted of a single helping and, as usual, he had finished first. Now, as he sat with his empty plate before him, Tostig drew him into the conversation.

'Are you fond of greenery, Thegn?' he enquired. 'A leafy bower on a sunlit afternoon: that kind of thing?'

'I quite like it, yes,' came the reply.

'Or perhaps you favour a shimmering meadow at midday, or even the lush pastures of early morn?'

'I hold them in equal esteem,' said Thegn.

'A very wise outlook.' Tostig paused for a long moment, then rose to his feet and took a stride towards the edge of the camp. 'Ah, greenery,' he murmured, gazing into the dull environs. 'To tell the truth, I've almost forgotten what it's like, we've been travelling for so many weeks. Nonetheless, we should view it as a deferred pleasure, rather than a lost one. Otherwise we risk losing all hope. Here we are in the midst of a stark and unforgiving land, deprived of light and existing on the most basic necessities. Daily we stumble over shale and flint, toiling onwards in the vague belief that at some distant time and place we'll see the sun rise again; and that spreading before us will be vast, hospitable ranges where the mules may finally be turned loose. Not until then will this struggle be done with. Odd to think, is it not, that success will only be confirmed when we can at last apply green ink to our map?'

No one answered, and for the next few minutes each man remained alone with his thoughts as the darkness encroached yet further. At some point during the conversation Snaebjorn had come and joined the others, having completed the many duties he undertook daily. Now he sat leaning with his back against a rock, eyes closed, apparently seizing the opportunity for a snatched doze. Ultimately, it was Thegn who ended the silence.

'I think I'll go and check the mules,' he announced. 'To make sure they've settled down after their crossing.'

'I've already checked them,' said Snaebjorn, without opening his eyes.

'All right, I'll wash the dishes instead.'

'I've done them too.'

'You didn't do mine,' said Thegn.

'You didn't ask,' Snaebjorn replied.

Thegn puffed out his cheeks, then stood up and buttoned his jacket. 'Well, I'll just take myself off for a stroll then.'

'Just a moment, Thegn,' said Tostig. 'Where are you going exactly?'

'To stretch my legs.'

'No, that won't do at all. They've been stretched enough for one day and, besides, I don't want you slipping away while we're in the middle of your hearing. You can retire to your tent until we call you, but don't go any further than that.'

'I assure you I won't,' said Thegn. 'Good night.'

'Good night,' chorused the others.

Tostig watched as his junior disappeared from view, then motioned towards Guthrum and Thorsson. Leaving Snaebjorn quietly resting against his rock, the three of them returned once more through the blackness to the makeshift court of justice. Here they sat and deliberated for many hours, with the lamp glowing above them at half-setting. Eventually Thorsson was sent to fetch Thegn. It took several attempts to wake him from his slumbers.

'Come on, my lad,' said Thorsson, when Thegn at last responded. 'Better get this over with.'

'Do I need my cap?' Thegn enquired.

'Yes, I should wear it if I were you.'

'Thanks, Thorsson.'

There was no sign of Snaebjorn, but a gentle tinkling of bells nearby suggested he had gone amongst the mules. Meanwhile, the tents flapped languidly in the breeze. Thorsson continued to wait as Thegn prepared himself.

'Hurry up,' he urged. 'This tribunal has cost us enough time as it is. You'll only weaken your position by dallying.'

'Sorry,' said Thegn.

A few minutes later he was standing before his three seated colleagues, the lamp shining brightly again. When all was ready, Tostig resumed proceedings.

'Well, Thegn,' he began. 'We have considered this matter long and hard; we've weighed you in the balance; and you'll no doubt be pleased to learn that we find you not guilty of conspiracy.'

'Thank you, sir.'

'It seems there was no case to answer.'

'I am indeed glad to hear it.'

'Instead you are charged with the lesser offence of gross insubordination. You will serve fourteen days in solitary confinement.'

Thegn opened his mouth as if to speak, then closed it again.

'However,' said Tostig. 'The sentence is suspended.'

Without further delay, the expedition continued north-ward, gradually moving away from the river. Snaebjorn took the lead. The day's journey was unremarkable, save for a small incident around about noon. During the brief twilight there was a whirr of wings high above them, as in the flight of a passing bird, and a moment later a sprig of foliage fell in their path. Snaebjorn saw it and picked it up. The sprig was withered and dry, but nevertheless its discovery brought encouragement to the entire party. All agreed that somewhere ahead the land must be green and fertile, and on this assumption they pressed forth with renewed vigour.

But, unknown to them, the bird had lost its way.

5

'SORRY TO INTERRUPT THE work, Mr Johns, but I think
we may have a problem.'

'Really, Scagg? Well, please come in and tell me about
it.'

'Do you want me to make myself scarce?' Chase
enquired.

'No, no,' said Scagg. 'It doesn't concern any of the men.'

'What is it then?' asked Johns.

'I thought you should know that one of the mules is
dawdling, deliberately it seems, and that this is having a
discouraging effect on the others. I've had it under observation all day, and several times I've noticed it dragging
the pace. Moreover, it comes to a complete halt at every
opportunity. If we allow it to carry on in this way, our
progress will be seriously disrupted.'

'You're quite right,' said Johns. 'Oddly enough, Chase
and I were just discussing our position, and we were wondering why we'd hardly got anywhere since yesterday. So
it's the mules to blame, is it?'

'One of them, sir.'

'One is enough.'

'So with your permission I'd like to administer some

discipline. A night under the hood should teach it a lesson it won't forget.'

'Have we brought a hood with us?'

'I took the liberty, yes.'

'Very well, Scagg. See to it, will you? And at the same time I suggest you treat all the other mules to a stick of barley sugar apiece. Then hopefully they'll see both sides of the coin.'

'Right you are, sir.'

After Scagg had departed, Johns turned to Chase and shook his head. 'Oh dear,' he murmured. 'The order for punishment is always the hardest to give.'

'So I imagine,' said Chase.

'That's why we've resorted to this so-called "modern" remedy of the hood. I'm told on good authority that it works and, frankly, anything more severe would serve no useful purpose in such a harsh climate: indeed it may even be counter-productive. Still, Chase, only time will tell. Now, where were we?'

'Discussing the wind, Mr Johns.'

'Ah, yes, the interminable wind. What's your analysis?'

'I'm afraid it bears very little moisture.'

'No likelihood of rain then?'

'Not for a while.'

'That is disappointing news,' said Johns. 'The last thing I want to do is impose water rationing; yet there appears little chance of locating any other source while we're on this scree. I had been assuming it would eventually ease out on to some verdant plain, criss-crossed by streams and rivers, but now I'm beginning to think that was just wishful thinking on my behalf.'

'Oh, I'm sure there's a flat plain ahead,' replied Chase. 'The way the wind sweeps unimpeded towards us has convinced me of that fact. Besides, we're almost down to sea level again.'

'Well, it's been such a struggle one would hardly believe we'd been descending for six days in a row. Listen to that gale, pounding the very walls of the tent as if it wants to tear them asunder. Will there be no relief?'

'I don't know, sir,' said Chase.

The flame guttered in the lantern as a fierce gust whirled through the encampment, striking one tent after another. Chase gathered up his charts and tables, and waited while Johns completed the latest entry in his journal. Then they buttoned their coats, extinguished the light and went outside. This sequence of events had become a nightly ritual. Next they would find their way through the blackness for a distance of about half a mile, following a northerly direction, carefully examining the ground and taking note of any landmarks or other points of interest. These were few in number. Nonetheless, both men agreed that their regular evening forays gave them a fair idea of the terrain that lay ahead, and thus prepared them for the following morning's march. Before returning they would always wait until their eyes had grown fully accustomed to the dark. Then they would retrace their steps back to their respective tents, each getting ready for bed without further recourse to lamplight. In this manner they helped conserve the supply of fuel.

* * *

'I can offer you a penny,' said Scagg.

'Pardon?' said Medleycott.

'For your thoughts.'

'Oh, yes, sorry, I was miles away.'

'So I observed. Is something troubling you?'

'Not really, no. Or shouldn't be anyway. It's just that today happens to be my birthday.'

'And you were thinking about Mrs Medleycott.'

'How on earth did you know that?'

'It's quite natural,' said Scagg. 'Everyone thinks of their mother on their birthday.'

'Do they?'

'Of course they do.'

Medleycott gave a long sigh. 'Yes, well, it's very true; and it's so unspeakably lonely out here that I can hardly bear it at times. This endless scree, this darkness, this pitiless wind: men have been driven to distraction by lesser torments. It's an utter wilderness. Do you know, I've been standing here for almost an hour gazing at absolutely nothing?'

'Which is why I came looking for you,' Scagg replied. 'You've been absent a good while.'

'Oh, I wouldn't have wandered far,' said Medleycott. 'I just wanted a few moments to myself, that was all.'

'But I thought you said you were lonely.'

'I remarked that this was a lonely place, yes.'

'Well, conducting a solitary vigil won't help matters, will it?' said Scagg. 'If it's your birthday then surely you should be with the other men, not stuck out here on your own. Now take my advice and get yourself back into camp before Mr Johns notices you're missing.'

'I'll go at once,' nodded Medleycott. 'Sorry, Scagg, that didn't even occur to me.'

'And many happy returns of the day.'

'Thank you.'

Scagg watched as Medleycott made his way towards the tents. He waited until he'd disappeared from view, then strolled in a purposeful manner around the margins of the camp, pausing at one point to inspect the mules. These were gathered together in a huddle with their backs to the wind, some sleeping, others eyeing him warily when he drew near. He glanced to his left. Tethered separately a short distance away was the single recalcitrant mule, its head concealed under a heavy linen hood just as it had been all through the night. Scagg stood and contemplated the scene for several minutes before moving on. Presently he came to the kitchen area, where Seddon was busy preparing breakfast. Here he paused again.

'Been in search of our early riser?' ventured Seddon.

'As a matter of fact I have,' Scagg replied.

'I saw him go by an hour ago. Sleepwalking, was he?'

'Yes, something like that.'

Scagg lifted the lid of the cooking pot and peered inside. Steam rose up to engulf him; quickly he replaced the lid. Next he poked around amongst the sundry stocks and provisions, opening boxes and closing them again. Finally he looked at Seddon and said, 'You've got plenty of flour, haven't you?'

'Plenty,' answered Seddon.

'Sugar?'

'Yes.'

'Fat?'

'Likewise.'

'I know for certain there's a bag of raisins somewhere,' Scagg announced. 'I loaded them myself. Got a baking tin?'

'Of course I've got a baking tin,' returned Seddon with indignation. 'What's all this leading up to anyway?'

'Well, Seddon,' said Scagg. 'I want you to pull off one of your culinary miracles.'

'Oh yes?'

'I'd like you to bake me a cake. Nothing special; just a simple cake with icing on the top. Can you do that for me?'

'I suppose so.'

'Much obliged. That'll be one I owe you.'

'I presume it's a secret, is it?'

'Correct,' replied Scagg. 'And don't worry about the candles: I'll see to them.'

'All right, when would you like it for?'

'Tonight.'

'Good grief,' murmured Seddon. 'You do want miracles, don't you?'

Without further discussion, Scagg glanced at his watch, then began his daily round of the tents, waking all those who were still asleep. First to emerge was Summerfield, whose turn it was to feed the mules. He was followed from the same tent by Plover and, lastly, Sargent. All were now clad in the full attire of surcoat and woolly helmet, and all walked with a kind of stoop as they headed out into the wind.

'Any idea when we're going to see some proper daylight again?' asked Sargent. 'All these early nights are taking their toll of me. Wearing me out, they are.'

'Is that why you're always last up?' Scagg countered.

'Who is?'

'You are.'

'It was only a civil enquiry.'

'Yes, well, I'm afraid the man to ask is Chase. He's been taking all the readings, not me.'

'Will it be days or weeks, do you think?'

'I expect it'll be one or the other,' said Scagg.

Sargent looked at him for several seconds through the opening of his helmet, then turned abruptly and walked off in the direction of the field kitchen. 'Get more information out of a stone,' he muttered, when he was out of earshot.

There was the usual gathering of breakfasters, all hunched together behind one of Summerfield's constructions while a gale raged around the camp. Sargent collected his helping of porridge and looked for a place to sit down. Finding nowhere suitable, he then wandered over to where Summerfield was still tending to his charges.

'You'd better hurry up,' he said. 'Or you'll miss your share of the vittles.'

'Not to worry,' Summerfield replied. 'Seddon always saves me something.'

Sargent nodded towards the hooded mule. 'Is that the one that's holding us back?'

'Supposedly, yes, although for my part I feel it's most unfair to blame the wretched creature for our shortcomings. Scagg has ordered me not to feed it until all the others have had their fill. Only then may I remove the hood, so he says.'

'Well, it's hardly a real punishment anyway,' said Sargent.

99

'Surely it would have been better to give it a sound beating and put it on half rations for a day or two.'

'I wouldn't let Mr Johns hear you talking like that if I were you,' rejoined Summerfield. 'In his opinion the well-being of the mules is our chief priority. Besides which, Professor Childish disapproved of those sort of methods.'

'Who's Professor Childish when he's at home?'

At these words Summerfield peered out of his woolly helmet with an incredulous expression on his face. 'But you must know who he was.'

'Was?'

'He's been dead for twenty years.'

'No wonder I've never heard of him.'

'For heaven's sake, Sargent! Professor Childish was the founder of Transportation Theory.'

'Transportation? Oh, you mean "Round 'em Up and Ship 'em Out!"'

'That's the popular name for it, yes,' said Summerfield. 'But I know privately Mr Johns prefers the term "transportation". Apparently he finds all the sloganeering rather distasteful.'

'Shocking,' agreed Sargent.

He sat down and stirred his porridge reflectively. Summerfield joined him, having now completed his duties. Meanwhile, at the opposite side of the camp, tents were already being dismantled.

'So this professor chap thought it all up, did he?' Sargent enquired at length.

'He did indeed.'

'I always assumed it was Johns' idea.'

'Well, certainly, Mr Johns had the technical means to carry the theory out; but it originated with Professor Childish. As a matter of fact, I've been studying his treatise lately, when I've found the time.'

'Yes, I've noticed you've had your nose stuck in that book most evenings.'

'It makes fascinating reading,' Summerfield continued. 'It's written in an archaic sort of style which takes some getting used to, but all the same it's absolutely brimful of ideas. I'm sure Mr Johns wouldn't mind if you wanted to borrow it after me.'

'I'll bear it in mind,' said Sargent. 'But to tell you the truth I don't really go in much for theories.'

'I take it you're not a subscriber then?'

'I'm not anything.'

'Then what on earth made you volunteer for such an arduous journey as this?'

'There was nothing else for me,' replied Sargent with a shrug. 'So I decided I might as well sign up.'

'Summerfield!' called a voice from the direction of the kitchen. 'Do you want this breakfast or not?!'

'Coming!' he called back, then, speaking to Sargent, 'Better dash.'

Summerfield sprang to his feet and in an instant he was gone. Sargent stayed where he was, spending quite some time finishing his porridge before eventually returning to the centre of the encampment. This was now a hive of activity. Most of the stores and equipment had been stacked ready for loading, the field kitchen was all folded away and the men were sorting out the last of their personal belongings. Only Summerfield stood stationary with his spoon and bowl as he hurried down a belated breakfast. Plover was near at hand. He was holding a small shaving mirror close to the lantern, looking at himself and making sure his woolly helmet was on straight.

'I'm surprised you're late, Summerfield,' he commented. 'Quite unusual, for you.'

'Yes, I know,' came the reply. 'I got talking to Sargent.'

'That must have been jolly interesting.'

'It was, actually,' answered Summerfield. 'I find him very good company.'

'Well, each to his own, I suppose.'

'Someone mention my name?' said Sargent, appearing out of the gloom.

'I was just saying you were on your own,' said Plover quickly. 'Now that Cook's no longer with us. Expect you're missing him, aren't you?'

'Why should I be missing him?'

'Because I thought the two of you were great pals.'

'We joined the expedition on the same day,' said Sargent. 'But I'd never met him before that.'

'Really? Well, I must say the two of you seemed to get on very well, sharing your plates, swapping jokes and so forth.'

'You mean we're birds of a feather?' said Sargent.

'Yes . . . er, no, of course not.'

'What then?'

'Well . . .'

'Plover,' intervened Summerfield. 'I think Scagg wants you for something.'

'Ah, does he?' said Plover. 'Then you must excuse me, gentlemen.'

Giving Sargent a curt nod, he smiled, then turned and walked away. After he'd gone, Sargent winked at Summerfield.

'Spoilsport,' he murmured, with a grin.

Sometime during that day, amongst his numerous other considerations, Seddon devised a means for baking a cake on an open stove. He refused to disclose the method to a curious Scagg, however, insisting on keeping it to himself. For his part, Scagg made sure Seddon received all the assistance he needed, and when the evening halt was called he instructed Blanchflower and Firth to help set up the field kitchen. There was nothing uncommon in this, as everyone was used to Scagg giving orders. What was noticeable, and remarked upon at different times by various people, was his increasing irritability as the new camp was established and supper prepared.

'What's irking him?' asked Sargent, after being snapped at for no apparent reason.

'I'm not sure,' replied Summerfield. 'It's rather odd, but he seems to be waiting for something. I've seen him glance at his watch once or twice as though he's due for an appointment.'

'Maybe Johns is going to make one of his speeches.'

'Yes, maybe.'

They followed Scagg's movements as he walked over to the kitchen and spoke to Seddon. Urgent words were exchanged, then Scagg went round informing everyone that supper was ready. This was quite unnecessary since supper was always eagerly anticipated by the whole party, most of whom had been hovering in the vicinity for the past half hour. The only exception was Johns, who delayed his appearance until precisely seven o'clock. Emerging from the 'command tent', as it had come to be known, he proceeded to his favoured place in the lee of Summerfield's stone dyke. Then, when the others had settled about him, the meal was begun. As usual on these occasions, talk was rare. The men ate in silence, apart from uttering scattered remarks which expressed how very agreeable the food was (Johns), or how it should have been cooked a little longer (Sargent). Afterwards everybody would be expected to disperse almost immediately. This evening was different, however, because all of a sudden Scagg rose to his feet and strode rather stiffly to the middle of the circle.

'Before we go to bed,' he announced, raising his voice against the ceaseless moan of the wind, 'I've one or two words to say to you all.'

As was his custom, Scagg was wearing his woolly helmet rolled up towards the crown of his head. During the past few weeks his beard and eyebrows had thickened, and these lent him a certain authority as he addressed his companions in the lamplight.

'This is a dark season,' he continued. 'Night and day are indistinguishable. We have endured a lengthy trek through perpetual gloom, and consequently some of us may have forgotten what time of year it is. In my case, only a chance conversation with Medleycott early this morning reminded me of today's date. Now, if you please, Seddon.'

At a signal from Scagg, Seddon entered the circle

carrying a large round biscuit tin. On his head he was sporting a chef's hat fashioned roughly from cardboard, and over his left arm was draped a white napkin. With a flourish he removed the lid from the tin, and revealed an iced cake dotted with a number of tiny candles. Some of the onlookers gasped in surprise.

'Oh, there was really no need,' said Johns.

'Certainly there was,' replied Scagg, clearing his throat before turning to face his leader. 'Mr Johns . . . er . . . may I call you William in these special circumstances?'

'Of course,' Johns affirmed.

'Well, William, as I say, it was only by chance that I remembered today is your birthday, and so, thanks to Seddon here, I am now able to present you with a celebratory cake, along with our good wishes. If you've no objection, we won't bother lighting the candles. I'm afraid the wind will just blow them straight out again.'

This last comment brought a round of laughter from the assembled men, followed by a robust chorus of 'Happy Birthday to You'. Then Johns offered his humble thanks and asked for the cake to be divided up so that everyone could have a share.

'No one must go to bed,' he insisted, 'until it's all gone.'

Smiling a rare smile, Scagg produced a knife and performed the honours. Only Medleycott declined a slice.

* * *

The process of civilisation is almost complete. We live our lives in safety and prosperity. Famine and disease have been defeated. Trade thrives everywhere. We no longer practise warfare and hence we have no need of a standing army. Neither do we fortify our cities and ports. For decades our navies have kept the peace by sailing along foreign shores and firing cannon-balls harmlessly into the sea. Diplomacy does the rest. There is no doubt that we've made the world a far better place to live in. Yet there remains one enduring problem: namely, the question of the mules. Since time immemorial they have been our inescapable burden. We have tolerated their presence simply because we have had no other option, but now, at long last, there is light at the end of the tunnel. The recent discovery of new territories in the north has offered a ready-made and welcome solution. We should seize it with both hands!

'You still reading?' enquired Sargent, from beneath his utility blanket.

'Oh, yes, sorry,' said Summerfield. 'I was thoroughly engrossed. Were you waiting to turn the light out?'

'Well, everyone else has been tucked up for a while now, so if you don't mind.'

'All right then. Sorry.'

Summerfield closed his book and put it away. Then he reached over, extinguished the lamp and settled down to sleep.

'Nearly finished it?' said Sargent.

'Almost, but to tell you the truth I'll be sorry to get to the end. The arguments Childish puts forward are utterly fascinating, and so original. What astounds me is that he wrote it more than twenty years ago yet we're only just beginning to put his theory into practice. I can't understand the delay.'

'The reason is obvious,' said a voice in the darkness. 'It's because he was ahead of his time.' The voice belonged to Plover.

'Oh, you're still awake, are you?' asked Summerfield.

'That question does not merit an answer. You were discussing Professor Childish, I believe.'

'Yes.'

'Well, fortunately the world has now caught up with him. All those eyebrows raised at the very mention of transportation have disappeared; all those do-gooders holding back progress with their moral doubts; all those heads stuck in the sand. The objectors have been silenced. Finally we can turn our attention to changing the theory into fact, and not a moment too soon in my opinion.'

'I had no idea you were such a zealot.'

'Well, it's not allowed, is it?' said Plover. 'Johns sees himself as the only "thinker" in the party and if the rest of us don't agree with every word he says we earn a black mark from his trusty lieutenant, Mr Scagg.'

'Oh, I think that's a bit harsh,' said Summerfield. 'Johns has always listened to what I have to say.'

'Lucky you.'

'So what's your particular gripe then?'

'Merely that we're not driving the mules hard enough. Johns is obsessed with all this welfare and general molly-coddling and as a result he's allowing them to dictate the pace. We should be miles further along by now.'

'But the whole purpose of this expedition is to find out

if the mules can survive the journey. There's absolutely no point in pushing them beyond their capabilities.'

'Come, come,' rejoined Plover. 'Have you never read Younghusband's pamphlet on the subject?'

'I'm afraid not,' said Summerfield. 'I'm only familiar with Childish.'

'Good grief, not another theory,' murmured Sargent.

'No, not another theory,' said Plover. 'The same one but with a completely different emphasis. Younghusband referred to what he called the "natural strengths" of the mules, and suggested they're far tougher than they lead us to believe. Laziness is what we used to call it, but of course Johns won't allow such expressions.'

'Well, yes, we do have one lazy mule,' conceded Summerfield.

'They're all lazy!' snapped Plover. 'They do nothing unless they're constantly spurred on; therefore spur them on we must, and if one or two fall by the wayside then so be it! In my judgment, all this talk about whether they can survive the journey is academic irrelevance. Our primary aim should be to take them to the Furthest Point from Civilisation and leave them there. What happens to them after that is no concern of ours.'

'But surely the theory should be put to certain tests before any lasting decision is made.'

'Not in my opinion,' said Plover. 'There's nothing more to discuss.'

At that the conversation subsided. The men lay silently in the darkness, and one by one drifted off to sleep. All except Summerfield. After tossing and turning for almost an hour, he eventually sat up and folded his utility blanket.

Then, taking care not to wake his companions, he picked his way to the entrance of the tent. Emerging into the cold air, he buttoned his surcoat and pulled his woolly helmet over his head. Summerfield passed the rest of the night wandering round the edge of the camp, occasionally calling to check on the mules, or adding new stones to the dyke he had built earlier. In the end he sat down behind it, out of the wind, and remained there, dozing quietly, until Seddon appeared and began preparing breakfast. It was Blanchflower's turn to feed the mules, so he was the next to surface, accompanied by Firth, who came along to lend a hand. In this desultory manner the entire camp gradually returned to life until everyone had risen and was out and about. Chase was particularly busy this morning. Leaving the tents far behind, he went up on to the high ground they'd descended the previous evening and took some readings. Then he reported to Johns. A short while later the assembled company heard an announcement.

'I have a piece of good news,' said Johns. 'I'm pleased to tell you that we can expect a glimmer of light at noon today.' He paused while the men cheered heartily, and then continued. 'It won't be much because the sun will barely nudge the horizon, yet at least we'll be assured that spring is on its way at last!'

There were further encouraging signs to come. Soon after the march had resumed, the terrain began to level out, seemingly on to the great plain that Chase had predicted. It was still stony underfoot, which made the going difficult, but nevertheless the expedition advanced with a much lighter step than before. Moreover, the mules appeared to have recovered some of their vigour. Instead of having to be cajoled along in the normal manner, they now proved easier to lead, practically breaking into a trot as they followed in Summerfield's wake. He in turn forged ahead, his body bent against the wind as he led the way into the unknown. The rest of the party had long since become accustomed to losing sight of him early in the day (despite Johns's reservations) and not seeing him again for several hours. Consequently, they were taken by surprise when just before midday he came back to meet them, emerging suddenly from the gloom with an ecstatic look on his face.

'There's a river!' he cried. 'I've seen it!'

He was holding his woolly helmet in his hand, and now, in his exuberance, he whirled it up into the air. In an instant it had been caught by a gust of wind, and quickly began tumbling away. Medleycott, who happened to be leading the mules, let go of their rope and ran back to retrieve the helmet. Instead of coming to a halt, however, the mules rushed forward in a bunch, taking their burdens with them.

'Get them under control, someone!' ordered Johns, when he realised what was happening.

Blanchflower and Firth ran up from behind, followed by Scagg, who roared instructions to everyone in sight. Summerfield had already set off in pursuit of the mules and made an attempt to grab their rope, but without success. Similar moves were tried by Chase and Medleycott. The stampede was now gaining momentum, resulting in sundry items falling from the mules' backs as they careered pell-mell towards their apparent objective: the river. A wide black ribbon was gradually taking shape in the darkness ahead of them, and with it there came the sound of water flowing. Next moment the leading mules were plunging in, dragging the rest behind them. Immediately the entire troop, all roped together, was being swept downstream. Without hesitation, Medleycott threw himself into the river and began swimming, though still fully clothed.

'Use your knife!' yelled Scagg. 'Cut the rope!'

Others were now in the water too, wading into the shallows to salvage various pieces of gear that had come adrift. Meanwhile, Medleycott had reached the mules and was at work with his knife amid the pandemonium. Panic had now taken hold, and despite his efforts he only managed to cut five mules free. With a struggle, the men brought four of these ashore. The rest continued to be pulled along with the flow of the river and were soon lost from view. With them went Medleycott. Summerfield ran along the bank shouting at him to swim back, but he still seemed intent on rescuing the mules. Finally he too vanished. Summerfield stumbled on until his legs would carry him no further.

'Medleycott!!' he howled in desperation. 'Come back!'

He stopped and for a long time stood motionless, staring into the distance. Presently Johns appeared beside him and placed a comforting hand on his shoulder.

'I fear we've lost him,' he said.

'Is there nothing else we can do?' asked Summerfield.

'I don't think so. This river is obviously more powerful than it looks. He'll be a mile away by now.'

While they'd been talking, a soft gleam had begun gradually to spread across the southern horizon. For a minute the land all about them was bathed in a pale silver light, but the figures on the river bank paid no heed and very soon it was gone again. By the time they'd walked back and rejoined the others, Scagg had started taking stock of the remaining supplies and equipment. The four surviving mules were being looked after by Blanchflower and Firth, while Seddon assembled what was left of the foldaway kitchen. The windbreak had gone, as had most of the pots, but the stove itself was still intact. Immediately, Summerfield set about building a stone dyke for Seddon to work behind. Two of the three tents had been recovered, soaking wet, from the river, and these had been unfolded so they could dry out. Much else was missing, including a substantial quantity of food. Johns ordered a simple hot meal to be cooked for everyone. Then, after a period of rest, he organised parties to follow the river in each direction in search of a suitable crossing place.

'It's our last hope,' he announced.

Plover, Sargent and Summerfield took the downstream leg. Keeping close to the bank, they peered constantly into the black water on the off-chance that Medleycott would still be found. Nothing was seen, however, and after a while they began to conjecture about what Johns would likely do next. It was a lacklustre conversation consisting mainly of Sargent giving his opinion that they had no choice but to turn back. When informed that this was out of the question, he appeared not to hear and merely repeated his assertion, at which point the others ceased to contradict him. Then suddenly a nearby scuffing noise brought them all to a halt.

'What was that?' said Plover.

Just ahead of them a dim shape was moving.

'Medleycott!' proclaimed Sargent.

'No, no,' said Summerfield. 'It's a mule.'

At the sound of their voices, the shape came closer, and a moment later they saw that it was indeed a mule, a young female, trailing a short length of rope. Sargent sprang forward in an attempt to grab it, and instantly the mule moved away again.

'I recognise that one,' announced Summerfield. 'It's the dawdler we punished under the hood. Poor Medleycott must have managed to cut it free before the current took him.'

'Well, three of us should be able to catch it,' said Plover. 'It'll be a good trophy to take back to Johns. Let's have a go.'

Nonetheless, despite their efforts, they repeatedly failed to get anywhere near the mule. Time after time they moved within a few yards of it, only to lose sight again as it vanished into the darkness. A quarter of an hour passed and still they'd had no success.

Then Summerfield said, 'Let me make a suggestion. I've had a few dealings with this one already. If you two go back to the camp, I'll try to coax it in on my own.'

'So that you can earn all the praise?' said Plover.

'Of course not,' responded Summerfield. 'I simply think it's the best workable solution; otherwise we're going to exhaust ourselves fairly quickly. What's your view, Sargent?'

'I agree with you,' came the reply.

A few minutes later Summerfield was walking alone

along the river bank. Quite soon he came upon the mule and at once paused. The mule did not move so he took a careful step forward. Then another. Then he stopped. Deliberately he turned away and gazed at the river. Still the mule remained where it was. Summerfield allowed several seconds to pass before again facing his quarry. The mule was now looking directly at him and appeared to be quite calm, yet when he tried edging forward it skipped away in a playful manner. Then it turned towards him once more. Summerfield waited.

'Come on then,' said the mule. 'Catch me if you can.'

There was a long leaden silence, broken finally by Summerfield.

'How dare you speak to me!' he uttered.

'What of it?' asked the mule. 'Just because you forbid us to talk do you think we'll lose our tongues?'

'I don't make the laws,' Summerfield replied. 'Even so, you had better be silent or you'll make things even worse for yourself.'

'What could be worse? I've already spent a night under that hood.'

'You can forget the hood. You're asking for a severe beating this time.'

'I don't think so,' answered the mule. 'You wouldn't lay a finger on me. You're far too civilised for that.'

'Maybe so,' said Summerfield. 'However, that doesn't mean I can restrain my companions. Some of them are less tolerant than me.'

'Then you'll just have to be my protector, won't you?'

* * *

Meanwhile, the other party had returned to the camp with some favourable news. Chase, Blanchflower and Firth had discovered a natural ford about a mile upriver, and they had succeeded in getting across and back quite easily. Their find was still under discussion when Summerfield appeared, leading the mule.

'Ah, Summerfield, well done,' said Johns. 'Come and join us. Tie it up, will you, Sargent?'

'Yes, sir.'

'I'd rather you didn't tether this one,' interceded Summerfield.

'Whyever not?' Johns enquired.

'Because I promised her she wouldn't be tied up any more.'

'She?!' snapped Scagg. 'Since when have we referred to mules in that manner?!'

'Admittedly never.'

'So what's the game then?!'

'It seemed the most practical approach,' said Summerfield. 'I really don't see what other option I had.'

'Of course you had an option!'

'It's all right, Scagg,' said Johns. 'I think Summerfield can be forgiven under the circumstances.'

'But it's outrageous making bargains with a mule!'

'I know, Scagg, I know. All the same, I'm afraid we're going to have to learn to live with it. An hour ago we thought we only had four mules left. Now we have five, and this one's a female, which is a bounty for us. It makes it worthwhile to continue our journey. Therefore we can allow a small concession.'

'Very well, sir,' murmured Scagg. 'If you say so.'

Accordingly, the mule was led away to join the others. Then Johns gathered the men around him and set forth his plans.

'Disaster has struck,' he began. 'Yet we shall not be defeated so readily. Blanchflower and Firth, I want you to return southward and collect the extra supplies. Go only as far as Summerfield's Depression: Cook should be there to meet you by now. In the meantime, the rest of us will take advantage of Chase's Crossing, as I propose to name it. With our limited resources we're going to make a "dash" for the Furthest Point. I think you'll all agree that we owe it to Medleycott to press on.'

'Of course,' said Plover.

The remnants of the afternoon were spent in making preparations for the following day. Scagg went through the food supplies and worked out a system for rationing, assisted by Seddon. The two remaining tents, having dried quickly in the wind, were now erected. It had been decided that Blanchflower and Firth would rest overnight before leaving, which meant there would be four in one tent and five in the other. At the end of the evening, in sombre company, Johns made an entry in his journal:

I regret to report that today we lost Medleycott in a tragic and costly accident. It should be recorded that he gave his life attempting to save some of our mules.

Despite the shortage of accommodation, Scagg arranged that Johns would have sole use of the command tent for one hour each day, immediately after supper. The purpose was to 'allow Mr Johns a little bit of peace and quiet', as

Scagg put it. During this period everyone else was expected to crowd into the other tent. Johns was quite prepared to receive visitors, however, and two nights after the river crossing he was playing host to Summerfield.

'I've come to return your book,' said his guest. 'Thank you for the loan: it was most interesting.'

'Interesting?' replied Johns. 'Does that mean you weren't entirely convinced by the arguments?'

'No, no,' said Summerfield quickly. 'It's just that I've become a little concerned about one aspect of the theory.'

'What's troubling you exactly?'

'It's about this homeland we're hoping to establish for the mules.'

'Yes, what of it?'

'Will they be treated fairly, Mr Johns? I mean, we're transporting them to the Furthest Point from Civilisation and leaving them there. Can we be sure they'll be able to cope on their own?'

'Frankly, we can't,' said Johns. 'There are many unanswered questions still remaining and everyone is aware of the risks. Nevertheless we had to begin somewhere. As you know, the aim of this expedition is to discover whether the mules can survive the initial journey. Our success will be the lodestar: the model for future advances. If the place is considered suitable, then the process of settlement will begin at once. Naturally, we'll need to provide basic sanitation; we'll also set up supply lines to help them through the first few seasons. After that, they'll be left entirely to their own devices.'

'But if all fails they'll suffer terribly!' exclaimed Summerfield.

'That's why we're only starting with a small number.'

'But . . .'

'Look, Summerfield, you must appreciate that even I have certain reservations about this, but I'm afraid there is no other option. The alternatives have been tried and none of them work. Let me assure you that I bear the mules no personal ill-will whatsoever. I would be the first to declare that most of them are honest and harmless creatures. They have no very deep dye of turpitude. Instead, their inherent weakness lies in all that they lack: the ability to make rational judgments; the concept of propriety; the power of self-discipline. They lose their heads far too easily: the incident at the river was a perfect demonstration of that. Furthermore, they do nothing profitable; they are strangers to industry; they don't invent things; they don't plough the waters of the deep; they don't extract minerals, construct bridges or dig tunnels. Neither do they have any understanding of science. As for art, well, yes, I admit they are capable of some wonderful creations in paint and clay; they possess a marvellous sense of colour; yet they only do this as a sort of pastime, never in a formal, studied way. Then, of course, they have their fanciful beliefs and superstitions, most of which defy all reason.'

Johns paused and gave a long sigh before continuing.

'Summerfield, I cannot overstate the efforts that have been made to let the mules live alongside us. Every conceivable solution has been tried, and every one has failed. Simply put, the mules are completely immune to the forces of civilisation; therefore, we have decided that the only answer is to allow them to develop separately in their own corner of the world; to build shelters and eke out some kind of pastoral existence. Believe me, it will be for their own good in the long run.'

'To quote Professor Childish.'

'Indeed.'

'Did you ever meet him?'

'Sadly, no,' said Johns. 'He had done all the hard work long before I was around.'

'Any notion of what he was like?'

'A real footslogger, apparently, but to start with it was mainly uphill. He first began to promulgate his ideas through a series of minor publications, followed by an extensive tour of lectures and public meetings. Then came the book, which famously received dreadful reviews. From the outset he was severely castigated; his proposals were considered unthinkable, offensive even; but gradually, as time passed, the Theory started to catch on. An early death left his work incomplete, but others soon picked up the baton, notably Younghusband and Clark, who quickly became the leading lights. It was they who came and built the blockhouse, of course, paving the way for those who followed. Unfortunately none of their mules survived the sea journey, so they didn't venture inland. That was in the closing decade of the last century, before the details had been properly thought through. Eventually a great conference was held, attended by many interested parties, including myself.'

'And Tostig.'

'Yes, Tostig was there too, so I'm told. I've never met him either. Not even an introduction, would you believe? As a matter of fact, I got the impression my presence was being ignored generally, so I didn't bother with the second conference they held the following year. Not that it made any difference by then. The main achievement of that first conference was its success in agreeing coordinates for the Furthest Point from Civilisation. It took days of debate and discussion, but finally an accord was reached. All further talk seemed superficial to me, so I just left them to it and got on with the job.'

'"Time for Action not Words."'

'Yes, indeed.'

Johns nodded and smiled at Summerfield, then began leafing through the pages of the newly returned book.

'Tell me, Summerfield,' he said, without looking up. 'How do you find the new system of rationing?'

'It appears to be working well enough,' replied Summerfield.

'Have you had to tighten your belt yet?'

'Not yet, Mr Johns, but I'm quite prepared to do so if necessary.'

'And does that go for all of your companions as well?'

'I'm sure it does.'

A moment passed before Johns spoke again.

'I hope you've noticed that the mules' allowance has not been reduced.'

'Yes, I must say I've noticed.'

'On this occasion it's the men who have made the sacrifice.'

'Yes.'

'So you see we do treat them as fairly as we can.'

6

WITH THE PASSING OF time, the days became gradually lighter. Spring was returning. The members of the eastern expedition, alerted by Thorsson, had paused to witness the long-awaited gleam in the southern sky, since when they had emerged from their rocky wilderness on to a broad windswept plain where they could find their way much more easily, although for the most part darkness still predominated. Tostig had chosen to mark the change in terrain by establishing a staging post for their return journey. Here were deposited some quantities of dried food, some water, and various pieces of equipment. Also three of the five pocket tents. The plan was to travel as lightly as possible for the final outward leg, Thorsson having calculated that the Agreed Furthest Point was at last within reach.

'Odd to think, is it not?' said Tostig. 'That by our own definition we are now beyond the scope of civilisation.'

He was lying side by side with Guthrum in the first pocket tent. The second tent was occupied by Thorsson and Snaebjorn, while Thegn slept alone in the supply tent, crammed amongst the bare necessities.

'Odd indeed,' replied Guthrum.

'And it highlights a dilemma of mine,' Tostig continued. 'Namely, the matter of the green ink.'

'What's your quandary?'

'Simply this, Guthrum. The nearer we get to our destination, the less the likelihood of finding the haven we're searching for. Oh, I know I haven't mentioned it to the men, but, let's admit it, the evidence is far from encouraging. This blasted wind hardly suggests the kind of climate we seek, and there has been absolutely no hint of greenery since we came across that sprig of foliage.'

'A false sign if ever there was one.'

'Quite,' said Tostig. 'Which brings me to the green ink. We have one bottle and it remains unopened. The bottle weighs the same as a day's ration of dried food for five men. The purpose of our march is to discover a sort of green oasis, and the purpose of the ink is to illustrate it on our map. Yet there seems little sense in carrying the ink when it probably won't be used. Far better to leave it behind and take an extra ration instead.'

'But if there's no green haven then our journey becomes pointless.'

'My dilemma in a nutshell.'

Tostig gave a sigh and fell momentarily silent. Outside in the blackness, bells could be heard tinkling as two or three mules sought shelter in the lee of the tent. (Tostig's mules remained untethered at night.)

'Shall I shoo them away?' asked Guthrum.

'No, leave them where they are,' said Tostig. 'There's nothing out there that can do them any mischief, and all the food is safely stowed with Thegn. Let them sleep where they wish.'

'Very good, sir. Now, with reference to your dilemma.'

'Yes?'

'I take it you have no intention of turning back?'

'Correct.'

'Then in my view there's only one solution.'

'Really, Guthrum? Well, tell me: I'm all ears.'

'It lies in the simple fact that the map must be finished, come what may. As far as the expedition is concerned, it makes no difference what we find at the AFP, whether it be oasis or desert. Either way, we cannot return home without a complete record of our journey; therefore, the ink will have to go with us.'

'You're right, of course, Guthrum, and very well put, if I may say so.'

'Thank you.'

'Remind Snaebjorn to include it when he loads up tomorrow. In the meantime, we must prepare ourselves for another kind of disappointment: the possibility that Johns may have beaten us to our destination.'

'Is it likely?'

'I've no idea,' said Tostig. 'Nonetheless, it merits serious contemplation. If he has indeed overtaken us, then he will have proved his route to be the faster of the two. This in turn will bring him all the benefits of priority; and for us, nothing. Because without question, Guthrum, there's much more to it than the simple matter of planting a flag.'

'I don't doubt it.'

'Imagine for a moment that the Theory turns out to be workable; that just beyond the horizon there lies a land which fully meets our requirements. It follows that the person who gets there first will not only receive all the credit, but also stands to rake in a handsome profit when the process of resettlement begins. Think of the lucrative contracts waiting to be won: the shipping, the supply lines, the transit camps. No wonder Johns has made such a race of it!'

'You don't believe his motives are altruistic then?'

'Oh, I'm certain his original intentions were beyond reproach,' declared Tostig. 'I've read several of his published articles and it's clear he shares our desire to return the mules to their natural state. Even so, there's no denying that he's persistently trodden an independent course: not once has he co-operated with the other interested parties; nor has he asked for their assistance. Johns is a true man of enterprise, but like other great explorers he is also flagrantly self-seeking. In his case, I'm afraid ambition has achieved the upper hand.'

'All the more reason to get there before him,' remarked Guthrum.

'Indeed, yes,' said Tostig. 'We must put these misgivings to one side, apply ourselves fixedly to our journey, and disregard Johns altogether. We have succeeded so far by treating this venture as an exercise in its own right, concentrating on the day-to-day logistics rather than some glorious moment of arrival. And thus we will continue. We have excellent equipment, ten healthy mules and just enough provisions to attain our goal. Furthermore, our teamwork has been first class.'

Here Tostig paused and corrected himself.

'First class, that is, with the exception of one person. One person who doesn't seem to understand the meaning of teamwork. You know, Guthrum, if it wasn't for our vigilance he could have let the side down on more than one occasion. Sometimes I'm tempted to put him on a diet of hardtack for a week, just to make him buck his ideas up.'

Outside the tent the bells had ceased jingling. The only sound was the beating of the canvas in the wind. The little camp lay silent.

Guthrum coughed and cleared his throat. 'Would you mind, sir, if I made a personal observation?'

'No, of course not. What is it?'

'Well, I think you tend to be a little hard on the lad.'

'Oh?' said Tostig. 'You surprise me.'

'Considering this is his first voyage, he's come forward in leaps and bounds,' Guthrum continued. 'He's diligent and hard-working, and also quite courageous. It's true he makes mistakes now and again, but haven't all of us in our youth?'

'I suppose so.'

'There are many I know who would be pleased to count him as one of their own. He has an "uncle", for example, who I'm sure has very good reason to be most proud of him.'

'Really?' said Tostig, his tone of voice brightening noticeably.

'And I can tell you that Thorsson also shares this opinion.'

'Thorsson is a man of exemplary judgment.'

'Indeed.'

'Well, well, Guthrum. It appears I may have underestimated our recruit.'

'Hardly a recruit any more, sir. He's been with us almost twelve months now, including the sea journey.'

'Why, yes, twelve months! How the time has flown!'

After a moment's quiet thought, Tostig suddenly sat up in his bed and lit the lamp. As light filled the tent, he reached for his pea jacket and searched through its pockets, eventually finding what he was looking for. Then he extinguished the lamp again. Finally he addressed his companion in the darkness.

'Guthrum,' he said. 'You remain my trusted Number Two.'

'Thank you, sir,' came the reply.

Tostig was first to rise next morning, even before Snaebjorn, and when the others emerged they found him bustling around the encampment, having already fed the mules and put the pan on for breakfast. He seemed to be in a cheerful mood, undaunted by the ferocious wind that continued to show no sign of abating. With still another hour until dawn, he allowed a lamp to be lit during breakfast (this meal was usually taken in complete darkness) and the men enjoyed the rare luxury of some potted marmalade. Immediately afterwards, he announced that he would like to make a small presentation.

'Come forward, will you, Thegn?' he entreated.

On this day, for the first time since the party had left the coast, Tostig's flag had been unfurled. It flapped in the wind at the top of a slender pole, close to where Tostig was standing. As Thegn approached, he reached for his hand and shook it firmly.

'Now then, Thegn,' he said. 'Guthrum tells me you've served with us for twelve months.'

'Eleven months and three weeks,' Thegn replied.

'Well, I think we can call it the full twelve amongst our select company. Are we all agreed on that?'

'All agreed,' said Thorsson.

'And in view of this,' resumed Tostig. 'I'd like to take the opportunity of returning your silver star.'

He produced the star and handed it to Thegn; then leaned forward and kissed him ceremonially on each cheek. This was followed by a smart salute.

Thegn stood holding the star in the palm of his hand, staring at it blankly.

'Have you any words to say to us?' asked Tostig.

Thegn did not speak.

'Thegn?'

'Oh, yes, sorry,' he said at length. 'I'm just quite aston-ished, that's all.'

'But you've seen it plenty of times before,' said Tostig. 'What's so astonishing about it?'

'I don't mean the star itself.'

'You mean what it represents?'

'No,' said Thegn. 'I mean it was a surprise.'

Again he fell silent.

'A salute will do as well as a speech,' murmured Guthrum.

'Of course,' answered Thegn, snapping quickly to attention and saluting.

Tostig looked him up and down.

'Good,' he said. 'Very good.'

Thereupon the little gathering dispersed, the tents

were folded and preparations for departure were begun. The bulk of the work was completed in less than half an hour. A short while later, Thegn was fixing his star on to the front of his navy cap when Snaebjorn approached.

'Welcome back to the fold,' he said, by way of greeting.

'I didn't know I'd left it,' replied Thegn.

'I've come to inform you that Tostig has just issued a new order.'

'Oh yes?'

'He says conditions have become too rough for normal headgear. Accordingly, all members of the party must abandon their caps in favour of woolly helmets. I take it you've brought one along, have you?'

'There's one in my pack.'

'Then you should unpack it immediately. I'm afraid this means you won't be able to display your silver star.'

'You won't be able to display yours either,' said Thegn.

'Mine makes no difference to me,' answered Snaebjorn, and with that he turned and walked away.

The last task to be carried out before leaving was to exchange a ration of dried food for the bottle of green ink. The ration was added to the depot they were leaving behind. Then, with woolly helmets on their heads, the men led the mules into the north.

'Did you hear?' said Tostig. 'In the dead of night did you hear a kind of wailing?'

'Actually I did,' replied Guthrum.

'And you assumed it was a trick of the wind?'

'Yes.'

'So did I,' rejoined Tostig. 'I thought it was the relentless moan of those great gusts as they came rolling across the plain. Yet as I lay on the verge of sleep I began to realise that the sound was quite specific to this camp of ours. Then the truth dawned on me. What I could hear wasn't the wind playing in the guy ropes: it was voices; and moreover it was voices I hadn't heard since my childhood. Tell me, Guthrum, have you ever known the mules to sing?'

'Never.'

'Well, I have. It was years and years ago, in that bygone age when they were regarded as a quaint minority, and when we scarcely took any notice of them. Occasionally, and for no clear reason, we would hear odd snatches of song coming from their dwellings, sung in a sombrous tone that bore no resemblance to anything else we'd heard. As I say, I was only a child at the time, but I recall their songs possessed the same mournful quality as that wailing we heard in the night. They danced as well, so I was told, swaying from side to side and gyrating like drunkards; but I never saw any of that.'

'How extraordinary,' said Guthrum.

'Eventually, of course, all such behaviour was quelled, and I haven't heard those voices since. Not until last night, that is.'

'What do you think's got into them?'

'I don't know,' said Tostig. 'Perhaps this desolate country has made them despondent and they've sought solace in the customs of their forebears. It's only natural, I suppose; they've nothing else, have they?'

'Maybe we should start keeping a closer eye on our hapless charges.'

'I think you're right, Guthrum. The last thing we want is for them to lose heart and falter at this stage in our journey. Also, I wonder if we shouldn't begin tethering them again at night.'

'For their own safety?'

'Indeed.'

'I'll see to it.'

'Curiously enough,' continued Tostig. 'At quite an early juncture Thegn mentioned that the mules might become troublesome as we neared our goal. "They might create problems for us" were his precise words. I remember dismissing the idea out of hand, but now it appears he may have had a point. Evidently his worries were far from groundless and actually served to display a good deal of common sense in the boy. It seems I learn something new about him every day.'

Tostig and Guthrum had ascended a steep bluff that rose a hundred feet above the plain. It was almost noon and the wind had lulled. Below them they could see their three companions: Snaebjorn was preparing a light meal while Thorsson did his calculations and Thegn attended to the mules. These were standing roped together in a line, passively awaiting their feed. To the south a faint trail disappeared into the gloom. To the north lay further emptiness.

'A fine view,' said Tostig.

'Or not much of one,' replied Guthrum. 'Depending on your outlook.'

'I suppose this absence of wind is little more than a brief hiatus?'

'So says Thorsson.'

'More gales imminent?'

'Apparently.'

'No promise of a few warm zephyrs to ease our way?'

'No.'

'Pity.'

They gazed into the distance for a while longer. Then, having seen enough, they returned to join the others. Tostig went straight over to Thegn.

'How are the mules' appetites?' he enquired.

'Interesting you should ask,' said Thegn. 'They're feeding well enough but they're certainly taking their time over it. Quite a solemn affair, actually. One would almost think it was the last meal they ever expected to get.'

Some of the mules had now ceased eating and were looking across at the two men.

'They were singing in the night,' Thegn added.

'You needn't concern yourself with that,' said Tostig, nodding towards a particular mule. 'See the one at the front there? Am I correct in thinking it generally leads the column when we're on the march?'

'Yes, it does.'

'Well, from now on make sure it receives an extra quantity of mash each day. Not too much, you understand: just enough to cause the rest of them to be jealous. With luck, it should take their minds off feeling sorry for themselves.'

'Right you are, sir.'

'As for the separate question of our own rations, I'm afraid each of us will be getting by on short measures for a day or two until the deficit is made up.' Tostig glanced at the dwindling supplies before smiling grimly to himself. 'And all for the sake of a little green ink.'

As Thegn resumed his duties, Tostig consulted Thorsson about their estimated position. Thorsson mentioned that the bluff would be the first noteworthy addition to the map for quite some while. It was the only landmark for miles around, and he suggested it should be given an official name. Tostig liked the idea but could think of none suitable, so at lunchtime he threw it open to the others.

'What about "Observation Point"?' offered Guthrum.

'But we hardly observed a thing,' said Tostig. 'The horizon was obscured.'

'All right then: "Obscurity Point".'

'Too vague.'

Guthrum puffed out his cheeks and gazed up at the looming bluff; but he said no more.

'I propose calling it "Solitude Point",' said Thorsson.

'Not bad,' said Tostig. 'How about you, Snaebjorn? What do you think?'

'Solitude Bluff.'

'An interesting variation. Why, all of a sudden we seem to have the makings of a parlour game on our hands. Come on, Thegn: your turn.'

'We could simply name it after whoever saw it first.'

'And who was that?'

Nobody answered.

'Come, come,' said Tostig. 'Let us not be coy. Surely one of us is able to claim the first sighting?'

For a full minute he looked from face to face, but still there were no takers.

'Well, gentlemen,' he said at length, 'I must confess such reticence makes me feel very proud indeed. Any one of you could have put yourself forward, but instead you each allowed your companions the chance. This speaks volumes about the comradeship that has developed between us all; furthermore, it provides the answer to the question under debate: Thorsson, next time you're working on the map you can mark this place as "Modesty Bluff".'

'Yes, sir.'

The issue being settled, they quickly completed their meal and prepared to continue the journey. A bleak afternoon was in store. Even as they departed the wind returned, streaming in from the north and bearing with it fine flecks of swirling dust: something they had not encountered before. There was mounting disquiet as it got into their eyes and throats, causing untold delays and raising doubts about the adequacy of the water supply.

'It is imperative that we find a river or spring soon,' said Tostig, when they retired that evening. 'Otherwise thirst will become a major problem.'

'The mules seem to be suffering the most,' said Guthrum. 'Their pace has slowed significantly.'

'Oh, I don't think that's caused by the weather.'

'Really?'

'No, Guthrum, I'm afraid they're displaying all the signs of self-willed torpor. It's a condition Younghusband identified years ago. As a matter of fact, he published a pamphlet on the subject. Basically his argument is that in times of hardship the mules tend to channel all their energies into their emotions, rather than any sort of physical activity. You're aware, of course, how strong they can be when they choose?'

'Indeed,' said Guthrum.

'So just imagine all that strength expressed in a show of sorrow. We heard it in the wailing that went on the other night: a crying out, I presume, for some god or other to come and help them. Well, we know there's no such thing as any god: we can only be saved by our own exertions, and the same applies for the mules, whether they like it or not.'

'What are we going to do then?'

'Simply plod on, Guthrum. We've already tried cajoling them with a regime of unfair feeding, but Thegn tells me their leader steadfastly refused the extra quantity on offer. Very well then: we'll have to employ other methods. I'm reluctant to be harsh, but if necessary we'll get behind them and drive them with sticks for the last few miles!'

Early next morning, Snaebjorn looked in through the flap of the supply tent where Thegn lay curled.

'Are you asleep?' he asked.

'Not now, no,' answered Thegn.

'Well, may I ask you something?'

'If you wish. Squeeze in.'

Snaebjorn entered and sat down on a wooden box. A layer of dust covered his clothing.

'Still the same out there then?' Thegn enquired.

'And thickening,' replied Snaebjorn, before lapsing into a prolonged silence.

Eventually Thegn said, 'What is it you want to ask me?'

'Just this,' said Snaebjorn. 'Why didn't you claim the first sighting of the bluff?'

'Because I wasn't sure if it was me or not.'

'But it must have been you. You led for most of the time yesterday morning.'

'That doesn't mean incontrovertibly that I noticed the bluff before anyone else. Come to think of it, I might ask why you didn't claim it. No doubt your eyesight is superior to mine.'

'Maybe so,' said Snaebjorn. 'Nonetheless, I'm convinced you saw it first.'

'Then go and report me to Tostig!' snapped Thegn. 'Have me charged with high treason or some such nonsense like you did the last time!'

'That was different,' murmured Snaebjorn. 'On that occasion I was only doing my duty.'

'What's all this about then?'

'Merely that I seem to have misjudged you.'

'Oh.'

'I assumed you were only included in the expedition because of your "connections", whereas I can now see that you possess certain valuable qualities.'

'Really?' said Thegn. 'Well, I won't ask you to list them.'

'Thank you.'

'Is that all you had to say to me?'

'Yes.'

'Then consider the matter settled.'

After Snaebjorn had withdrawn, Thegn lay for some minutes gazing at the roof of the tent. His face at first bore a bewildered expression, but eventually this disappeared and was replaced with a smile. He gave a quiet laugh and shook his head; then he got up and went out. Snaebjorn was busy making breakfast, and neither man paid the other any attention. Tostig and Guthrum were standing near the group of mules, studiously watching them take their feed. Throughout the night a restless jangling of bells had permeated the little camp, and as the wind shook the flimsy walls the mournful singing had been heard again. It had lasted for many an hour, and only with the breaking of dawn had the voices fallen silent. Now the mules were eating, gathered together in a half-circle, heads bowed, facing away from the men, and seemingly oblivious to the flying dust.

'Odd,' remarked Guthrum. 'They usually put their backs to the breeze whenever they get the chance.'

'Yes, but you know how fickle they can be,' said Tostig. 'Frankly, nothing in their behaviour surprises me any more.'

'Here's Thorsson.'

'Ah, the navigator returns.'

Thorsson had been out on the open ground taking some readings. Now he returned with news that the Agreed Furthest Point was less than five miles away. 'We should arrive there around noon,' he added. 'Then I'll be able to confirm the exact position more accurately.'

After breakfast, Tostig announced that lots would be drawn to decide who should carry the flag, and therefore who should have the honour of planting it at their destination.

'In so doing we'll avoid the kind of restraint we witnessed at Modesty Bluff,' he explained. 'I don't want everybody holding back and saying "after you" at this stage in our journey; otherwise, we'll never get anywhere.'

In the event the winning lot belonged to Thegn, who mumbled his thanks but said little else when the flag was given him for safekeeping. Then camp was broken and the expedition pressed on. During the past hour the dust storm had worsened. This hampered progress considerably. With visibility little better than in the dark days of winter, frequent stops had to be made while Thorsson checked they weren't straying from their correct course; and after every stop it became increasingly difficult to get the mules moving again. Snaebjorn had taken over from Thegn, but even he was having a struggle managing his charges (there were no sticks on hand with which to drive them). As the morning advanced, however, the gale occasionally subsided, allowing the dust to disperse and offering the travellers a brief glimpse of what lay ahead. It was always the same: a vast, desolate wilderness stretching away towards the horizon. With evident weariness, they covered yet another mile. Then Thorsson spoke to Tostig and a halt was called. It was almost midday. Beneath a leaden sky, Thorsson produced his compass and did some calculations in his notebook. He glanced to the north and to the east, before turning and giving Tostig a nod.

'This is it,' he said.

'The Agreed Furthest Point?'

'Yes.'

There followed a lengthy silence, during which Thegn thrust the flagpole disconsolately into the ground. Immediately the standard unfurled itself and began flogging violently in the wind. The men stood around gazing blankly at one another. Meanwhile, the mules raised their heads and set up a great, sorrowful wailing; swaying back and forth, they rolled their eyes to the heavens in an outpouring of abject despair. For a long time Tostig remained motionless, apparently lost in thought. He looked first at the mules, then at the land he had brought them to. Finally, he spoke.

'This is a terrible place,' he said. 'They cannot possibly live here.'

7

'YOU KNOW WHAT I'D like?' said Sargent.

'No,' replied Seddon. 'Do tell us.'

'I'd like a plate of freshly baked scones.'

'Oh yes?'

'Scones served piping hot with lashings of butter and jam. A bit of cream would be nice as well, just to finish the job; but the main thing is they'd have to be freshly baked.'

Sargent was reclining on his utility blanket with his hands behind his head. He watched as the tent billowed languidly in the wind, causing dappled lamplight to play along the walls.

'I'm afraid scones are off the menu for the time being,' remarked Seddon.

'No spare flour then?' said Sargent.

'No flour at all,' came the answer.

The tent had four occupants. Sargent was in his normal position by the door. Next to him was Summerfield, already fast asleep. Then came Seddon, and at the far end was Plover. The latter had adopted his usual pose. He was lying on his side, outstretched with his legs crossed and his head propped on one hand, facing the doorway.

He waited a moment and then said, 'I think you'll find that the correct pronunciation is "scones".'

'"Scones?"' repeated Sargent.

'"Scones,"' repeated Plover.

'Well, I've never heard that before. We've always said "scones" where I come from.'

'Same here,' agreed Seddon.

'I assure you the word is "scones",' said Plover. 'You should look it up when you get the opportunity.'

'Yes, I will,' rejoined Sargent. 'When I get the opportunity.'

He reached over to the lamp and turned it off. In the neighbouring tent a muffled conversation could be heard, indicating that Johns, Scagg (and possibly Chase) were still awake. Sargent also seemed keen to continue talking.

'No flour, eh?' he said.

'Not an ounce.'

'Biscuits?'

'A few.'

'Beans?'

'Likewise.'

'I suppose there's still plenty of the patent malt drink?'

'Yep,' confirmed Seddon. 'The entire case was saved from the river.'

'Well, there's a mercy.'

'Don't you like it then?'

'I didn't mind it at first, but to tell the truth I've had that much of the stuff it's beginning to swill round inside me.'

'So you won't mind when we start dishing it out to the mules.'

'What?!'

'We gave them the last of their mash this evening,' said Seddon. 'The rest was washed away in the disaster.'

'Are you telling me they're going to be sharing our rations?'

'According to Scagg, yes.'

'Blimey.'

'You should be quite pleased: it'll give you something else to moan about.'

'Oh, I fully reserve the right to moan,' said Sargent. 'It's the only pleasure I get these days.'

A series of grunts and curses in the darkness signalled that he was finally getting ready to bed down for the night, and within a few minutes he was snoring. The other tent had now gone quiet.

'Tell me, Seddon,' said Plover. 'What's our exact position regarding the supplies?'

'Quite precarious,' Seddon answered.

'It's going to be a close call, isn't it?'

'Indeed.'

'I thought as much,' Plover sighed. 'What a damned fiasco this is.'

Not until several seconds had passed did Seddon respond.

'Pardon?' he said.

'Well, don't you think so?' said Plover.

'Think what?'

'That this expedition has been a complete shambles from start to finish. Look at it: we've had one catastrophe after another: supplies running out; mules crushed or drowned; men strung out in one's and two's across half a continent; perfectly good tents abandoned; the list goes on and on.'

'And you could have organised it better, could you?'

'I'm just saying . . .'

'Look, Plover!' rasped Seddon. 'I've told you before, I'm not interested in your weaselly sort of griping!'

'But Sargent complains morning, noon and night,' protested Plover.

'That's different! Sargent is a time-served whinger of long-standing, and what's more it's a privilege he's earned. In your case, if you've got anything to say you can say it directly to Mr Johns. Otherwise I suggest you keep your mouth well and truly shut!'

The snoring had ceased.

'Who?' said Sargent, drowsily.

'Nothing,' replied Seddon. 'It was a disturbance over nothing.'

There was no further talk.

Outside, under the open sky, the five surviving mules were sleeping. Ever since the incident on the river, they had been allowed to shelter between the two tents at night, rather than being confined to the edge of the camp. The four males were tethered together in a group; the sole female, unrestrained, nestled amongst them. And so they remained for the long, cold hours before dawn, at which time Seddon emerged and started cooking breakfast. He was accompanied by Summerfield, whose usual duty was to prepare hot mash for the mules. This having run out the previous evening, however, he instead gave them a simplified version of the men's rations. He then joined his comrades to eat. The morning was a dismal grey, and full daylight was very slow in coming. Consequently, it was not until the equipment was being packed up and loaded did anyone notice that the female had at some point slipped away. She was eventually spotted loitering some hundred yards to the west, and Summerfield was sent to fetch her back.

He advanced without hurry, setting off in a casual manner as if embarking on a country stroll. The mule appeared to ignore his approach, her attention seemingly otherwise engaged; but when he drew near she moved out of reach again. Summerfield paused. He could now see what was occupying her. She was toying with a smooth blue pebble, the size and shape of a small egg. Sometimes she tossed it up and down, or weighed it in the palm of her hand; sometimes she rubbed it against her skin, carefully examining the blue stain it left behind. Still Summerfield did not stir, but continued to regard her in silence. Finally, curiosity got the better of her and she glanced across at him. With a faint smile on his face, Summerfield reached into his pocket and produced a similar pebble.

'Snap,' he said.

'Snap yourself,' said the mule.

He held his pebble towards her. 'Would you like this?'

'I don't mind.'

'Catch then.'

After catching the pebble and comparing it with her own, the mule then apparently lost interest in both and let the hand holding them fall idly to her side.

'Did you have enough to eat?' Summerfield enquired.

'Just about.'

'Good.' He smiled again. 'Ready to go then?'

'Who?'

'You.'

The mule stared at Summerfield and said, 'I do have a name, you know.'

'Oh. Yes. Of course. What is it?'

'You didn't think I had a name, did you? You just thought I was one of those "wretched mules". The pretty female.'

'Well . . .'

'Gribble.'

'I'm sorry?'

'That's my name. Nice, isn't it?'

'Yes,' said Summerfield. 'Gribble. Yes, it is very nice. Now we really should be thinking about moving.'

The mule ignored this comment. Instead she said quietly, 'Your friend came and spoke to me last night.'

'What friend?'

'Peewit.'

'Ah,' said Summerfield. 'You mean Plover.'

'We call him Peewit.'

'He's not really a friend. Just a travelling companion.'

'He told me I should watch my step. He said I'd do well to remember which side my bread was buttered.'

'Yes, that sounds like Plover. Well, don't worry about what he says. He has no authority.'

'I told him it wasn't buttered either side.'

Summerfield laughed. 'Very good, Gribble. Yes, that's very good indeed.'

'I wouldn't laugh too loudly,' she replied. 'Grim the Collier is watching us.'

She nodded in the direction of the camp, and Summerfield turned to see Scagg standing some distance away, observing proceedings.

'Why do you call him Grim the Collier?'

'On account of his big black beard.'

'Oh, I see.'

'And we call your leader Dock.'

'What about me?' said Summerfield. 'Have you given me a name too?'

'No,' answered the mule. 'We haven't.'

'Maybe you will after a while.'

'Maybe.'

Again Summerfield glanced towards the camp. Even from this distance it was evident that most of the gear had been packed and loaded. Soon it would be time to leave, yet he was making little headway with the mule.

'Your leader doesn't allow us any buttered bread,' she said.

'No, he doesn't,' acknowledged Summerfield. 'Nevertheless, your welfare is of great concern to him.'

'But we live our lives dressed in sackcloth!'

'That is a simple matter of expedience; generally speaking you're not treated badly at all. Mr Johns sees to it you're sufficiently fed and watered; and as for the sackcloth, you should actually consider yourself fortunate: in some societies mules are made to wear bells around their necks.'

'And that makes me fortunate, does it?'

'Now listen, Gribble!' snapped Summerfield. 'I've been patient with you so far, but I must tell you you're seriously pushing your luck. You've already won a major concession in not being tethered at night, yet you continue to be troublesome. Now what's brought this on exactly?'

'My burden is too great.'

'But you already carry less than the others.'

'It's still too much.'

'Well, it can't be helped. You must at least shoulder your fair share.'

'For what purpose?' said Gribble. 'So that you can take us to the back of beyond and leave us there?'

'How on earth do you know about that?' demanded Summerfield.

'Because I'm not stupid!'

'Summerfield!' came a cry from the encampment. 'What's keeping you?!'

It was Scagg.

'Nothing of importance!' Summerfield called back. 'Give me another minute, will you?!'

'All right, but we need to get going shortly!'

'You heard him,' said Summerfield to the mule. 'Now do come on or you'll get left behind.'

'What about my burden?' she asked.

'I'll do everything I can to get it reduced. It may not be straight away but I promise I'll try. Now, please, can we make a move?'

'I suppose so.'

'Follow me then.'

Without further debate, Summerfield turned and headed back towards the main group. Gribble trailed in his wake, still clasping her blue pebbles. She passed under the critical eye of Scagg, who shook his head but said nothing when Summerfield selected a few lightweight items for her to carry. Soon afterwards the signal to depart was given. United again, the five mules fell into line one behind the other, and the expedition resumed its northward course. Johns was keen to take advantage of the gradually improving light, which had been of great help recently despite the shortages and the ceaseless gales. The days were brief in length, and chiefly overcast, but compared to the weeks of perpetual darkness the situation had improved no end. In this respect, said Johns, they could commend themselves.

'Our original plan is at last approaching fruition,' he told Scagg that evening. 'As you know, the idea of the winter journey was so we would reach our destination at the start of spring: the best time of year to establish any kind of settlement. Obviously the success of that remains in the balance, but at least it now appears likely we'll arrive when we said we would, which is most gratifying.'

'"The light at the end of the tunnel,"' offered Scagg.

'Indeed yes,' said Johns. 'Day by day we're getting a clearer picture of the type of landscape we're set to encounter. A blank canvas, I suppose one might call it, on which we hope to make a mark.'

'I'm sure we will, sir.'

'Thank you, Scagg. Your support has been quite invaluable.'

'Have you come to any conclusions about the settlement itself?'

'Only dim ones, I'm afraid; but we must always live in hope. Now I wonder where Chase has got to. He said he was just going out to stretch his legs, but he's been absent a good half hour.'

'This sounds like him now.'

Some boots scuffed outside; then the tent flaps parted and Chase entered.

'Sorry about the delay,' he said, when Johns glanced at his pocket watch. 'I detected a change in the atmosphere, a sort of heaviness, and I've been trying to define exactly what it is.'

'The possibility of rain?' enquired Johns.

'Sadly, no, sir,' replied Chase. 'Rather a dry element, as a matter of fact.' He held out his sleeve to show them. 'The air is laden with dust particles,' he explained. 'This is a mere half hour's worth.'

'Dust!' said Johns. 'The last thing we need!'

'Blowing down from the north, too,' Chase added.

They listened as the canvas thudded laboriously in the wind.

'We seem to be under constant siege by harsh external forces,' remarked Johns. 'Yet I wonder how we'd feel if we woke tomorrow and heard the gentle pitter-patter of rain on the roof? Homesick beyond measure, I don't doubt.'

Carefully, Chase brushed his clothes and swept the dust outside; then he clambered into his own corner of the tent and got ready to go to sleep. 'It's the morning dew that I miss,' he said.

'Really, Chase?' said Johns. 'So you're a bit of a romantic at heart then?'

'Not really, sir,' came the reply. 'But normally when it's dewy in the morning it turns out nice later.'

'There's not much chance of that happening round this place,' put in Scagg. 'The weather's always horrible.'

'I suppose it's why no one's bothered coming here before us,' said Johns. 'Apart from our friend Tostig, of course.'

'Tostig?' said Chase. 'Oh, yes: I'd forgotten all about him. I wonder how he's getting on.'

'Same as we are, probably,' murmured Scagg.

Thereafter the discussion subsided. Chase and Scagg settled down quietly beneath their blankets, and within minutes the forlorn roar of the night had lulled them both into deep slumbers. Johns, though, stayed awake a little longer. For a while he sat motionless, his journal in his hand, gazing at the flickering lamplight. Along with the rest of his comrades, he had now grown a beard: not a grizzly one like Scagg's, but, nonetheless, one that showed he'd been travelling for many weeks. It had been an arduous time. Behind him were stacked the depleted remains of his once-vast range of equipment. His men were tired. The fabric of the tent was worn thin, and, outside, the flag was in tatters on its flimsy staff.

Johns's reverie ceased when a sudden draught of air caused the lamp to flare up momentarily. He glanced down at his journal. Then, opening it on a new page, he took his pen and wrote:

Morale very good despite worsening conditions. Latest hazard has arrived in the form of flying dust. Most unwelcome.

Inadvertently mentioned Tostig this evening during talk with men. Hope it does not prove to be an unlucky slip. Feel we are nearing our goal and should hate for them to be disappointed.

At the close of the following day, just after supper, Johns asked for Summerfield to come and see him in the command tent. He arranged for Scagg and Chase to make themselves temporarily absent, then sat and awaited his visitor.

Summerfield was prompt. 'You wanted to see me, Mr Johns?'

'Yes, Summerfield, do come in out of the cold.'

'Thank you, sir.'

Summerfield entered and removed his woolly helmet.

'Now, Summerfield, I'm not going to beat about the bush,' said Johns. 'It's about this mule. The female.'

'Oh yes?'

'You seem to have won her trust.'

'I've tried to, yes, sir. I thought it might be of benefit to the expedition, given the circumstances.'

'Really?' Johns considered the explanation for some time. 'Yes, well I suppose I can understand your line of reasoning,' he resumed. 'The problem is, Summerfield, that in the past we've always kept the mules very much at arm's length.'

'I know, sir.'

'Yet I've been reliably informed you've been conversing with this one, and have even gone so far as to give her a name.'

'Actually, sir, she already had a name.'

'Good heavens!'

'They all have names,' said Summerfield. 'She's called Gribble, which quite suits her, I think. And you remember the one who was crushed under the tugboat? That was her brother: his name was Thrip. Then she lost two cousins in the river. They were called Vetch and Madder. And the four . . .'

'Summerfield! Summerfield!' interrupted Johns. 'What on earth are you trying to prove by all this?'

'Nothing, sir.'

'But you know very well you're not supposed to have dealings of any sort with the mules, not even to talk to them, let alone learn their family history!'

Summerfield bowed his head. 'I'm sorry, Mr Johns, and I hope you can forgive me. I know my conduct must appear somewhat aberrant. It's just that over the last few days I've come to see qualities in the mules I thought only we possessed: humour, companionship and so forth; and it's made me realise they're hardly different from ourselves.'

'Nevertheless, in the final analysis they *are* different,' said Johns. 'It's a scientific fact: their minds operate differently to ours; therefore, they behave differently. That's why we classify them as mules; and that's why they're being sent away.'

'And well they know it.'

'What?!' exclaimed Johns. 'I hope you haven't disclosed any details!'

'There was no need,' said Summerfield. 'They're not fools: they've already worked it out for themselves.'

Johns sighed and shook his head.

'Such a dreadful state of affairs!' he uttered. 'I really must insist you put an end to this fraternising at once. Apart from it being most unseemly, I fear you may be creating extra difficulties for all of us in terms of both discipline and control. Yes, Summerfield, I know you meant well, but it has got to stop immediately. Do I make myself clear?'

'Perfectly, sir.'

'Good,' said Johns. 'Then we'll draw a line under the matter.' He leaned back and smiled broadly at Summerfield. 'On a lighter note, you'll be pleased to hear that your cherished ambition will soon be within reach.'

A moment passed.

'Beg your pardon, Mr Johns,' said Summerfield. 'What cherished ambition?'

'Why, to be first to reach the Furthest Point, of course.'

'Oh that. Er . . . yes, I am quite looking forward to it.'

The smile disappeared.

'Quite looking forward to it?' Johns repeated. 'Surely you can summon up a bit more enthusiasm than that, Summerfield; after all, you've been our keenest trailblazer thus far.'

'I'm as eager as ever,' came the reply.

'Well, try to show it, can't you?' snapped Johns. 'It's not much to ask.'

'No, sir. Sorry. Will that be all?'

'For now, yes.'

'All right, then. Good night.'

'Night.'

Johns did not look at Summerfield as he headed outside. After he'd gone, however, he glanced towards the doorway. 'Damn and blast,' he murmured to himself.

The next morning dawned cold and bleak. In the south a dense bank of clouds obliterated the sunrise; in the north the sky was clear, but the air was flecked with incoming particles of dust. The two tents stood parallel to one another, with a space in between. The space was empty. When Seddon emerged he headed straight for the makeshift cooking area, buttoning his coat as he went. Struggling in the wind, he got the stove lit and put a pan on before turning back towards the tents. Only then did he notice the mules were missing. Immediately he went to the command tent and woke Johns, who rose quickly and initiated a search.

'They can't have got far in one night,' he asserted. 'The trouble is we don't know which direction they took off in.'

'Back the way we came?' suggested Scagg.

'Unlikely,' said Johns. 'They wouldn't want to cross that river on their own. Yet there are no obvious tracks going anywhere else.'

'They must have covered them over.'

'Possibly, Scagg; or more probably the dust did.'

'Mr Johns!' called Plover. 'There's one of them!'

He was pointing to the west of the camp, where a short distance away Gribble could be seen wandering slowly about, picking up pebbles from the ground, examining them closely and then discarding them again. She seemed oblivious to the hue and cry that was going on all around her, and showed not the slightest sign of being a potential runaway.

'Keep your eye on her, Plover!' ordered Johns. 'The rest of us will have to spread out and see if we can trace the others. We'll meet back here in one hour's time.'

Before proceeding, Plover went back into the tent and

exchanged his woolly helmet for the high-peaked cap he'd worn during the early part of the expedition. This gave him rather an official bearing, especially as he'd taken care to keep his beard neatly trimmed during the past weeks. With a determined stride, he marched out of the camp towards Gribble. She was now only a hundred yards away; he covered the distance in less than a minute. As he approached she turned her back as if she hadn't seen him coming, and moved a little further off. Plover followed, dogging her resolutely until at last she drew to a halt.

'Up to your usual tricks?' he remarked.

Gribble said nothing.

'I suppose you think you're very clever, don't you?' Plover continued. 'Helping the others to sneak off.'

'It wasn't me,' she replied.

'Who was it then?'

'Don't know.'

'Of course it was you,' he said. 'You were the only one who wasn't tied up. I knew you couldn't be trusted: we gave you an inch and look what happened. Well, you'll be sorry this time. They'll have a rope round your neck sure as I'm standing here, and that'll put an end to your fun and games.'

Gribble turned and peered towards the camp.

'Is breakfast ready yet?' she asked.

'No, it isn't!' retorted Plover. 'In case you hadn't noticed, everybody's busy seeking the rest of the fugitives. You'll just have to go without.'

'As usual.'

'What was that?'

'I said I'll have to go without as usual.'

'You get your full provender,' said Plover. 'What is it you imagine you go without exactly?'

'Comfort,' answered Gribble. 'Warmth; sympathy; kindness.'

Plover broke in. 'Oh, don't try making me feel pity for you,' he said. 'It just won't wash at all; your situation is of your own making and no one else's.'

'Our own making?!' she cried. 'How can you say that when you held us down for generations!'

'You held yourselves down!' countered Plover. 'It had nothing to do with us! The simple truth is that your ancestors sat idly in the sun, while ours toiled and sweated in preparation for winter. Then when they fell behind they put the blame on everybody but themselves. They curled up, covered their heads and hoped it would get better, which it didn't. Now you and your kind are paying the price: you were born feckless, and feckless you will always remain.'

'So we're being punished because of who we are,' said Gribble.

'Because of what you are,' answered Plover. 'And I tell you: the sooner you've all been shipped out the better.'

'Then you'll be happy, will you?'

'Life will be vastly improved, yes.'

'That's not what I asked.'

'Don't be impertinent!!' Plover raised his voice and instantly Gribble fell silent. For some moments the two of them glared at each other in open hostility; then Plover turned abruptly away and strode back to the camp. Gribble followed at a distance, having now lapsed into a wordless sulk. She passed the next hour arranging her collection of pebbles in a small pile. These numbered half a dozen, all blue in colour, and all roughly the same size. Meanwhile, Plover tinkered with the stove. Seddon had extinguished the flame when he went off to join the search party, and, try as he might, Plover was unable to get it going again. Eventually, he gave the priming mechanism a dismissive prod, as if to suggest it might be faulty, and turned his attention elsewhere. By this time one or two of his comrades were beginning to return. Chase and Sargent trudged in from the north-east, shaking their heads when Plover looked at them enquiringly.

'No success?' he said.

'Nothing,' replied Sargent. 'They've vanished completely.'

'That's put paid to the expedition then.'

'Not necessarily,' said Chase. 'We've still got one mule left so I expect Mr Johns will want to press on.'

'Shame the "one mule" is the most awkward of the bunch,' observed Plover.

'You can say that again,' agreed Sargent. 'A wily specimen and no mistake.'

'Here's Mr Johns now,' said Chase.

Johns had appeared in the distance, accompanied by Seddon. Beyond them could be seen the advancing figures of Summerfield and Scagg.

'Obviously no luck either,' said Sargent.

On entering the camp, Johns immediately asked Seddon to prepare a belated breakfast.

'Any food missing?' he queried.

'Not as far as I can tell,' answered Seddon, after sorting

through the stock of provisions. 'Oh, except for the bag of barley sugar.' He looked a second time. 'Yes, that seems to have gone.'

'Well, I don't know how far they expect to travel on a handful of sweets,' remarked Johns. 'What an infantile escapade! Don't they realise we're doing this for their sakes as much as ours?'

'Apparently not, sir,' said Seddon.

'They'll be sorry when they starve to death.'

While Seddon busied himself with his pans, Johns went over and spoke to Scagg.

'Yet another setback,' he said. 'Nonetheless, we still have one mule remaining; therefore, I intend to press on. I trust I have your agreement on this?'

'Certainly, Mr Johns,' said Scagg. 'I'm determined we'll get to the Furthest Point, come what may.'

'Good show, Scagg.'

A short time later Seddon announced breakfast.

'Sorry it's a little overcooked, gentlemen,' he commented. 'Someone's been fiddling with the stove and it was difficult to regulate properly.' As he said this he threw a glance at Plover, who gave no hint of having heard him.

Gribble ate separately at the other side of the camp. Summerfield took her food to her, and was a little while in coming back. When finally he returned his face betrayed anger.

'Plover,' he said. 'What on earth did you say to Gribble earlier?'

'I simply reminded her of a few harsh realities,' Plover replied.

'Such as?'

'Such as the fact that the mules have no future in the civilised world.'

'Well, I wish you'd been a little more tactful,' said Summerfield. 'Now you've gone and upset her.'

'Is this true?' asked Johns. 'You're sure she's not merely play-acting?'

'I'm afraid not, sir,' answered Summerfield. 'She really is quite distraught. Furthermore, she says she's lost the will to go on. She told me she can't possibly walk another step.'

'Can't or won't?'

Summerfield shrugged. 'There's not much difference.'

'Then we'll just have to put the whip behind her,' said Plover.

'I don't think so,' said Johns. 'That won't help matters at all.'

'What are we going to do then?' enquired Scagg.

'I'm not sure yet. We'll need to consider it.'

Accordingly, straight after breakfast Johns and Scagg went into the command tent for a consultation. They spent half an hour discussing the various options; then they called in Chase.

'Now then, Chase,' began Johns. 'It's about your instrument case.'

'Yes, sir?'

'I gather it's your personal property.'

'That's correct,' said Chase. 'The instruments have been in my family for years, as a matter of fact. I come from a long line of navigators.'

'So I'm given to understand,' said Johns. 'Actually, it's

not the equipment I'm interested in so much as the case itself.'

'Ah.'

'Looks like a nice piece of timber.'

'Finest mahogany.'

'Really?'

'Specially selected by the manufacturer.'

'Well, Chase, I was wondering if you would be prepared to sacrifice it for the good of the expedition? You see, we urgently need some timber and apart from a few discarded provisions boxes there's little else available. It would really help us if you'd consent to this; naturally your contribution would be noted in the records.'

'Of course, Mr Johns, you're most welcome to use it.'

'Thank you, Chase,' said Johns. 'Scagg here will provide you with some cloth to wrap your instruments in. That will be all. Can you send in Sargent next, please?'

'Yes, sir.'

A minute later Sargent arrived. 'You wanted to see me, Mr Johns?'

'Yes, Sargent. Now when you joined this expedition I remember you described yourself as a jack-of-all-trades.'

'Yes, sir,' replied Sargent. 'That's what I am.'

'And does that list of trades include carpentry?'

'I can do a bit of joinery, yes.'

'All right, well, we won't quibble over semantics.'

'Sir?'

'You can call yourself a joiner if you wish.'

'Thank you, sir.'

'What I want, Sargent, is for you to build me a kind of portable chair: something that can be borne by four

men, one at each corner. In ancient times such a con-
veyance was known as a litter. It needs to be as light as
possible, but strong enough to take Gribble's weight.
We've decided if she won't walk to the Furthest Point
then we'll jolly well carry her there! Do you have any
questions, Sargent?'

'None I can think of, sir.'

'Then you can start directly. Use whatever materials
you require.'

'Right you are, sir.'

After Sargent had gone, Johns turned to Scagg.
'There's one slight consolation arising from the loss of
the four mules,' he said. 'It means our rations should
stretch that little bit further. Heaven knows, we're going
to need all our strength in the coming days.'

Sargent spent several hours building his portable chair.
First he gathered together the few available pieces of
timber (including Chase's instrument case, now empty)
and laid them out on the ground. Then, when he'd
devised a basic pattern, he set to work. For most of the
time his companions left him undisturbed, instead seizing
the opportunity to complete minor tasks of their own.
Eventually, however, Plover wandered over to see how
Sargent was getting along. By this stage the litter was
halfway to completion.

'This is sheer folly,' Plover murmured, when he saw
it. 'The mules are supposed to be our bearers, not the
other way round.'

'I'm only doing what I've been told,' replied Sargent.

'I'm aware of that,' said Plover. 'Yours is not to reason why.'

'Exactly.'

'Well, so much for our "dash" to the Furthest Point. At this rate it'll take a month of Sundays.'

'Plover!' called Johns from the other side of the camp. 'Can I have a word, please?'

'I'll be right with you, sir!'

When Plover joined him, Johns asked, 'Why do you persist in wearing that high-peaked cap in these conditions?'

'Sorry, Mr Johns,' rejoined Plover. 'Actually, I forgot I was still wearing it.'

Johns looked him up and down. 'You always have to be different, don't you?' was all he said.

Some while later, as Johns and Scagg conferred over their notes, they were approached by Sargent. At first he went unnoticed and merely hovered awkwardly nearby. Finally, Johns looked up.

'Yes, Sargent?'

'It's about the handles, sir.'

'What about them?'

'We haven't got any.'

'Is there nothing to spare?'

'No, sir,' said Sargent. 'We're short of two stout poles. The chair needs one on each side, so it can be carried properly.'

'How long do these poles need to be?'

'About the same length as the tent poles, sir.'

Johns gave a sigh. 'Very well, Sargent,' he said. 'I suppose if you must have them you must.'

'But then we'll be down to a single tent!' objected Scagg. 'We can't sleep seven at a time!'

'I know, Scagg, I know,' said Johns. 'I'm afraid all of us will just have to take turns and get by as best we can.'

'If I could have the ridge pole as well, sir,' Sargent ventured, 'I could improve the basic frame.'

Ultimately it was agreed that not only were the tent poles to be sacrificed, but also a section of canvas, so the litter could be fitted with a canopy to protect Gribble from the weather. In addition it was to have an upholstered seat. This would be made separately by Summerfield, who had offered his services to help speed things up. The afternoon was swiftly wearing on.

'Clearly, we're not going to get moving until tomorrow,' said Johns. 'So we might as well draw up a sleeping roster beginning immediately. Can you see to that please, Scagg?'

'Yes, sir.'

In the event it was not until after dusk that the litter was finished. By this time, one or two lamps had been lit and the stove was on for supper. When Johns heard the job was done, he went and carried out an inspection, after which he congratulated Sargent and Summerfield for their fine workmanship. Then Gribble was brought over.

'Now, Gribble,' said Johns. 'We've built this so that you can travel safe and sound to our destination. Would you like to try it?'

Gribble said nothing, but silently parted the canopy and stepped on to the litter. Then she sat down and closed the canopy behind her. The men waited. From within there came a quiet cough. They all moved away slightly. A minute passed.

'Gribble?' said Johns. 'Gribble, do you like it?'

There was no reply.

'Gribble, why don't you come out and eat?'

Further silence.

'Looks as if she's turned in for the night,' suggested Scagg.

'All right, well, that's all the more supper for each of us,' said Johns.

When this comment brought no response, they gave up and left Gribble alone.

The new sleeping arrangements entailed five men occupying the single remaining tent, while two others waited outside. These 'nightwatchmen' were to be replaced hourly on a rotating basis until everyone had done a stint. The first names on the roster belonged to Seddon and Sargent, so when their companions went to bed they made themselves as comfortable as they could under their utility blankets.

'To tell the truth, it doesn't make much difference to me whether I'm inside or out,' declared Sargent. 'After the day I've had I could sleep standing up in my boots.'

'If I were you I wouldn't say that too loudly,' answered Seddon. 'It sounds like you're volunteering.'

'Me?' said Sargent. 'Volunteer? Never!'

During the succeeding hours the diminutive encampment underwent repeated onslaughts of wind and dust. Dust now lay thick on every surface: on the tent, on the stack of supplies, on the canopy of the portable chair; and it only served to worsen the already poor visibility. By general accord the lanterns were extinguished overnight, which meant each pair of watchmen fulfilled their spell in total darkness. This later resulted in a surprise for Sargent. Despite protestations from Scagg, Johns had insisted on having his own name included on the roster so that he could carry out his fair share of the duties. In consequence it was Johns who eventually emerged to relieve Sargent. His advancing figure was barely perceptible in the gloom.

'About time too,' growled Sargent, who hadn't bothered to examine the roster in detail.

'Good evening, Sargent,' said Johns. 'I believe I'm quite punctual, as a matter of fact.'

'Oh, sorry, sir. I didn't know it was you.'

'Who did you think it was then?'

'Er . . . not sure, sir.'

'Someone who can't tell the time, perhaps?'

'No, sir.'

'You really should be more careful what you say, Sargent,' observed Johns. 'I could have been anybody coming along.'

'Yes, sir. Sorry.'

'Sleep well, Sargent.'

'Thank you, sir.'

Meanwhile, Plover had made an appearance, relinquishing his place in the tent to Seddon.

'Ah, Plover,' said Johns, glancing up briefly.

There was little further conversation. If Johns noticed that Plover had reverted to his woolly helmet then he didn't mention it, and for his part Plover drew no particular attention to the fact. Instead they sat side by side, with their backs to the wind, and for the ensuing hour exchanged only occasional banalities. Next to turn out were Chase and Scagg. These two got on easily together, and passed the time discussing obscure geographical matters. They were followed in due course by Sargent and, lastly, Summerfield. Sargent was down-in-the-mouth, and complained at some length that the roster had been deliberately set up 'against' him.

'I'm the only one who's had to get out of bed twice,' he muttered. 'Typical of my luck.'

Summerfield attempted to argue that the situation was the same for everyone, and that over subsequent nights it would even out quite fairly; but his efforts were all in vain. Sargent had a simpler explanation.

'My card's been marked ever since we started this trip,' he said. 'It's always the same: wherever I go you'll find me at the bottom of the pile.'

'What about the mules, though?' demanded Summerfield. 'You're much better off compared to them.' His manner was unusually terse.

'Yes, Mr Summerfield,' replied Sargent. 'So I've often been told.'

Both men were now gazing at the dim outline of the litter, which stood some distance away, fully exposed to the elements. Its occupant had remained silent throughout the hours of darkness. Summerfield took a deep breath.

'Look, Sargent,' he said. 'I'm sorry I snapped at you like that: it's not your fault. It's just that I sometimes have very grave doubts about what we're doing here. Let's admit it, the Theory barely stands up to close scrutiny: a set of harsh measures disguised as ideology by some well-intentioned professor. I mean, what exactly does society hope to achieve by rounding up all the mules and shipping them off to the wildest reaches of the earth? Will it really bring improvement, or have we been fooling ourselves all along?'

Sargent gave the questions a few moments' thought.

'Don't ask me,' he said.

After that the subject was dropped.

When dawn finally came, nobody professed to having had a good night's sleep. Instead, they wandered around the camp, waiting for breakfast and becoming irritated with one another for scant reason. Johns mentioned to Scagg that he found this state of affairs rather disturbing.

'It's only the first morning,' he said. 'What will their mood be like when they've been carrying that chair for a few days?'

'They'll soon adapt to it,' Scagg answered. 'They always do.'

'Maybe we . . . good grief!'

Johns broke off as Gribble drew back her canopy and stepped out. The cause of his astonishment was clear. Since the previous evening Gribble's appearance had changed beyond recognition. She was still dressed in sackcloth, but now there was a belt fastened around her waist. This belt was made from a strip of canvas, and served to give her garment a degree of femininity formerly lacking. Also, her hair was elaborately plaited, whereas hitherto it had always been unkempt. Most striking, though, were the bright blue lines that ran across her face: two on each cheek, and one in a V-shape on her forehead. These lines had been applied in the form of a thick paste, apparently ground down from the blue stones so carefully chosen by Gribble.

'I wondered why she wanted that spare strip of canvas,' said Sargent, reddening slightly.

Apart from this solitary remark, the men seemed at a complete loss for words. They stood in a half-circle gaping as Gribble passed by before seating herself at a discreet distance from the cooking area. There she waited until Summerfield delivered her breakfast. When he rejoined his comrades he said, 'Gribble asked me to say she had a pleasant night, thank you very much.'

'Well, that's something,' replied Johns.

As departure time approached, great care was taken to ensure that only the most essential items were packed for the onward journey. Any gear considered dispensable was left behind in a new depot. The rest was bundled into three loads, along with the remaining food supplies. Then, when all was ready, Gribble was requested to take her place on the litter. She was to be carried on this first day by Chase, Seddon, Sargent and Plover, while the other three men shouldered the packs. 'Unexpectedly light' was the unanimous verdict when the litter was raised from the ground and they got moving. The air was heavy with dust, however, and it was not long before Gribble closed the canopy, leaving her entourage to battle on as best they could. After an hour, Johns called a halt.

'Slow but steady,' he announced. 'So far, so good.'

During the break, Chase was asked to check their position. Summerfield had been leading the way, and Chase quickly established that he had, in fact, erred from their desired course.

'We're a bit too far to the west,' Chase told Johns. 'An easy enough mistake.'

'Maybe so,' Johns replied. 'Yet I wouldn't have expected it from Summerfield of all people.'

'No, I suppose not.'

'He's seemed rather distracted of late; therefore, I think I'll take over the leading from now on, and I'll make sure to confer regularly with you.'

'Righto, sir,' said Chase.

When the journey resumed, no more comments were heard about the litter being 'unexpectedly light'. Instead the men fell into a solemn march, heads down against the wind, and kept their thoughts to themselves. In this manner they continued for the rest of the day. The miles dragged by, and there was little to distinguish one hour from the next. Occasionally Gribble would peek out from her recess as if taking note of their progress. Then her face would vanish once more. Otherwise she was rarely seen. At meal breaks it was always Summerfield who served her. Johns did not wholly approve of this arrangement but, as he said to Scagg, no one else ever offered to do it, so for the time being it might as well stand.

By dusk the pace had slowed noticeably. At six o'clock Johns paused and raised an arm. Immediately the entire party halted, unrolled the tent, and began setting up camp.

'Actually I was only adjusting my pack,' said Johns. 'But I suppose this is as good a place to stop as any.'

* * *

The days passed, and gradually their objective drew nearer. One morning, after breakfast, Sargent made a great show of inspecting the portable chair. He went from corner to corner, spitting on his hands before grasping each of the carrying poles to test the grip. When he'd finished he shook his head in a puzzled way, then wandered back to join his companions.

'What's the matter, Sargent?' Johns enquired.

'Well, it's very odd, sir,' came the reply. 'But it seems to be heavier at the front left-hand corner.'

'You mean the corner you were carrying all day yesterday?'

'Yes, sir,' said Sargent. 'I've tried all the other corners and mine's definitely the heaviest. I just can't understand it.'

'But you built the blasted thing!'

Sargent sighed deeply. 'I know, sir,' he said. 'That's the worst part of it.'

'Well, take another corner then.'

'No, it's all right, sir,' said Sargent. 'I'll keep my corner now I'm used to the weight. I'm just saying it's heavier than the others, that's all.'

'Sargent, would you like some chocolate?' said Plover suddenly.

Six startled faces turned towards him.

'Please don't make jokes like that,' Johns uttered. 'Not when we're struggling on short rations. You really should know better, Plover.'

'It wasn't a joke, sir.' Plover reached into his inside pocket and produced a complete bar of chocolate, still pristine in its wrapper. 'I've been saving this since the expedition began,' he said. 'I thought Sargent might enjoy a pick-me-up seeing as he's having to endure extra hardship. As a matter of fact, there's enough for everybody.'

A stunned silence followed, during which the bar was passed round amongst the men. It was divided into eight sections, and consequently there was one piece remaining at the end.

'Gribble can have that bit, if she wants,' said Plover.

'Are you sure?' said Summerfield.

'Of course I'm sure.'

'Would you like to hand it to her yourself then?'

'No, no. I'll allow you that pleasure.'

'All right, well, thank you, Plover. That's very nice of you.'

'Hear, hear,' agreed Johns. 'Well done, Plover. Very well done indeed, and it so happens you've chosen the perfect moment for such a gesture. Chase and I have been keeping this next piece of news quiet so as not to raise false hopes, but I feel under the circumstances it's safe to make an announcement. I'm pleased to tell everybody that we should reach the Furthest Point later today!'

At once a mighty cheer rose up, and the men all went round shaking hands with one another.

'On a cautionary note,' Johns added, 'I think I should warn you of the possibility that Tostig may have beaten us to it. Now, as I've said from the start, this is not a race, and personally it makes no difference whether he gets there first or not. Nevertheless, I know a few of you might find such an outcome difficult to accept. Therefore, you should prepare yourselves for disappointment.'

'What will we do if he's there to meet us?' asked Seddon.

'Congratulate him, of course,' Johns replied.

Gribble chose to mark the occasion by renewing her blue streaks (which Sargent referred to as 'war paint'). She seldom left the confines of her litter any more, but this morning she made a brief appearance as the men strove to pack away the gear. For a short while she walked amongst them, nodding and smiling from time to time, until at last the inclement weather drove her back inside. She spoke quietly to Summerfield before withdrawing, and was not seen again for some hours. Subsequently, all efforts were concentrated on the journey ahead. If Johns' prediction was to come true, they needed to get a move on, and everyone agreed that a smart pace was required. So it was that all of a sudden Chase, Sargent, Scagg and Plover grabbed hold of the litter and set off with it, leaving the other three labouring after them with the baggage. It turned out that this 'jape' had been secretly organised by Scagg, in order to maintain a light-hearted spirit in the face of hardship. Unfortunately, Johns did not seem to view it this way, since he was amongst those left behind, and when he caught up with the rest of the party his feathers were clearly ruffled. Saying nothing, he purposefully strode past them until he had reclaimed his position at the head of the column. Only after another hour did his indignation subside, at which time his comrades heard him whistling a merry tune.

'He's happy now,' remarked Scagg. 'We're on the home straight.'

Despite this optimism, there was one last hitch. With only a mile to go, the dust thickened considerably, and Johns found it necessary to stop and check his bearings with Chase. This took a minute or so. Then, when the men raised the litter to move off again, Gribble began rocking it violently, forcing them to put it down.

'Gribble, what do you think you're doing?' Johns demanded.

She opened the canopy and looked out.

'I wish to be borne aloft,' she answered.

'Don't be so damned silly,' said Johns. 'It's hard enough carrying you as it is without you being awkward.'

'Very well,' said Gribble, stepping nimbly out of the litter. 'I'm not going any further.'

'What?!'

'I wish to be borne aloft,' she repeated. 'For the last mile.'

Johns clasped his hands together and regarded her patiently.

'Look, Gribble,' he said. 'You really must try to be reasonable.'

'I can't be reasonable!' she snapped. 'I'm only a mule, remember. We don't do reasonable things! All I know is that your mission cannot succeed without me; therefore, I'll only go on if you agree to my wishes.'

They had come to an impasse, so Johns moved away and conferred quietly with Scagg.

'Why don't we make a grab for her?' Scagg suggested. 'Surely seven of us can manage that?'

'I'm not so certain,' Johns countered. 'We're all tired, whilst she's as fresh as a daisy, and very canny to boot. I doubt if we could get anywhere near her. Moreover, I'm reluctant to use coercion this late in the game. She's been fairly cooperative to date, and I'm inclined to give her

the benefit and find out exactly what these wishes are.'
He turned towards Gribble and addressed her directly.
'So you want to be borne aloft, do you?'

'At shoulder height,' she replied. 'For the last mile.'

'Yes, well, I suppose we can go along with that.'

'I want another cushion for my litter.'

'That can be arranged.'

'And I desire to be known henceforth as Princess
Gribble,' she continued. 'I wish to be granted full title
to all the lands hereabout, so that I can reign over them
for ever more.'

'What on earth are you talking about?' said Johns. 'You
can't stay here on your own.'

'I won't be on my own,' said Gribble. 'I'll be with my
consort.'

At these words the assembled men laughed in disbe-
lief. The laughter faded, however, when Summerfield
stepped forward.

'She means me, sir,' he announced.

'You, Summerfield?!' exclaimed Johns. 'Have you taken
leave of your senses?'

'I don't believe so, sir.'

'Are you telling me you intend to live in this place?
With this mule?'

'Yes, sir.'

'But it's quite unthinkable. I simply won't hear of it.
Even setting aside the moral question, which we won't
discuss now, there's the matter of feasibility. You must be
aware that our supplies have practically run out. What
do you suppose you would live on?'

'Supplies can be sent up,' Summerfield answered. 'It's

been known all along that establishing a colony would require outside support: you told me that yourself, sir. With me here there's a much greater chance of success.'

'And what about the months of adversity and darkness, the bitter cold, possibly even starvation?'

'We've endured pretty much already, Mr Johns. The worst is behind us.'

Johns gave Summerfield a thoughtful look. 'It seems you've considered this quite carefully,' he said. 'So when did the pair of you plan it all?'

'I've been visiting Gribble at night,' Summerfield explained.

'You mean . . . ?'

'Yes, sir.'

'I see.' Johns regarded Summerfield for a long moment before continuing. 'Well, Summerfield, I'm sure I'm not alone when I say this comes as a great shock. Heaven knows how I'm going to explain it in my journal. All the same I must admit your scheme does have its merits. It offers the chance to test the Theory of Transportation at an empirical level, thus achieving far more than our original goal. What's your opinion, Scagg?'

'I'd prefer to reserve judgment, if you don't mind, sir,' Scagg replied. 'But I should point out that this delay is costing us valuable time. There's hardly an hour of daylight remaining.'

'You're correct as usual,' said Johns. 'Yes, we really must hurry if we're to arrive before nightfall. All right, Summerfield, I think we can accept these demands in principle, although, of course, the details will have to be ironed out later. Now can you please ask "Princess Gribble" to board her carriage immediately?'

'Yes, sir.' Summerfield lowered his voice. 'By the way, sir,' he added. 'The royal title wasn't my idea, nor the bit about bearing her aloft.'

'Never mind that now,' said Johns. 'Let's just get moving, shall we?'

After a word from Summerfield, Gribble returned to the litter and stepped gracefully inside, closing the canopy behind her. Then she was raised to shoulder height and the journey commenced once more. It took a while for the men to adapt to the new posture, but fortunately the ground was flat and before long they'd got into their stride. The sky had begun steadily to darken, investing this final march with a sense of mounting urgency. Already Johns had gone to the front of the column, and with every step his lead increased further. In his hand he carried the battered flagstaff. Soon he was a good fifty yards ahead, pressing forward with a marked determination. He appeared to be counting his paces, and at a certain point he abruptly stopped and turned to wait for the rest of the party. Amidst the swirling dust he stood like a statue until the others joined him.

'Here we are at last,' he said, smiling.

The litter was laid down, Chase verified their position, and the men gathered around Johns to give him three cheers.

'Success indeed,' said Scagg. 'It looks as if we're first after all.'

He shook hands with Johns, followed in turn by each of the others.

Then, as night hastened on, the wind abated. Suddenly the dust cleared, revealing a mound of freshly dug earth with a flag stuck in the top. When Johns caught sight of it, he fell to his knees.

'Oh no!' he cried. 'No, no, no, no, no!'

8

TOSTIG SPENT TWO DAYS at the Agreed Furthest Point from Civilisation. During this time he and his men conducted a series of tests, in order to confirm his doubts about the possibility of settlement. They examined the soil to see if it would support basic cultivation (it would not) and they dug a well in the hope of finding water (there was none). They also carried out a brief meteorological study, whose results suggested a severe lack of rainfall in the region. Meanwhile, Thorsson put the finishing touches to his map, on which the area around the AFP was shown in a dull shade of grey. When it was ready he handed it to Tostig.

'With my compliments,' he said. 'A depiction of nothingness, complete in every detail.'

Tostig studied the map for some minutes before returning it to Thorsson as a keepsake. It was an accomplished piece of work, he explained, but there was no practical use for it. On the second day, Snaebjorn made an appraisal of the mules' health and general condition. Afterwards, the five strongest were taken to one side. The remaining five had their bell collars removed; then Tostig produced a revolver from his pocket and shot them dead.

Their bodies were thrown into the well. Deposited alongside them were a number of unwanted items, including the bottle of green ink. The place was marked with a mound of earth, and a flag. Tostig's final act before departing was to write a courteous note to Johns. This read as follows:

> Dear Commander Johns,
> As you see, we arrived and found little of interest. Stayed for two days. We now wish you a safe voyage home.
>   Kind regards
>   Tostig

The note was pinned to the base of the flagpole. Next morning, with nothing left to do, the eastern party started back the way they had come. Only Thegn glanced behind him as the camp was abandoned by the small procession of men and mules. His companions didn't bother, and consequently he was the last to catch a glimpse of the flag that had once been so precious to them all. Soon it had disappeared from view. Ahead of them lay the faint trail they had established on their outward journey: a collection of footprints, sometimes vague, sometimes clear, which rarely wavered from a straight line. As such it was a source of regret for Tostig.

'Quite a shame, really,' he said. 'I had imagined this trail of ours would develop eventually into a proper road teeming with traffic (though strictly one-way, of course). I envisaged a great thoroughfare running the full distance from the coast to the Furthest Point. Naturally, there would be numerous obstacles to overcome: for example, those huge boulders we encountered would present a challenge to even the most practised of engineers, not to mention the rapids we crossed. Nevertheless, we know the route is at least viable, and consequently it is disappointing to realise our exploits will come to nothing. There will be no road to the settlement. Instead, our tracks will succumb to the ravages of the wind and the dust, before finally vanishing altogether.'

'Will no one visit here again?' asked Guthrum.

'I doubt it,' Tostig replied. 'We've already proved the place to be uninhabitable, and we will report it accordingly. Having said that, however, there may come a time when other possibilities are thought up by enterprising individuals as yet unborn. Other schemes, other solutions. And then, who knows? Maybe a hundred years from now our steps will be retraced by men with ideas very different to our own.'

'"Explorers of the new century,"' suggested Guthrum.

'Quite so,' said Tostig.

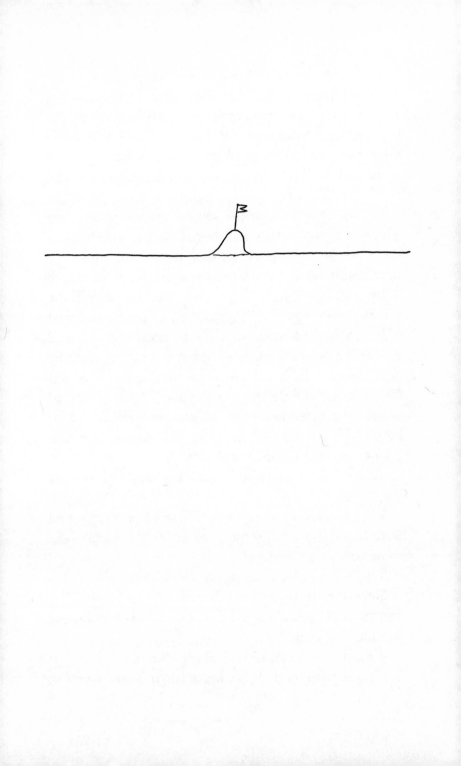

It was Snaebjorn who first detected the presence of the sea. The return party had been journeying for many weeks, and they were now wandering, gaunt and thin, along the dry river bed. Snaebjorn and Thegn were leading, while their three comrades lagged some distance behind.

'Look how bright the sky is,' said Snaebjorn. 'A sure sign that the sea is close at hand.'

Already they had passed several marker posts, each with its ragged pennant, and they knew they were nearing the coast. Snaebjorn's observation merely confirmed the fact. 'Thorsson would tell you the same thing,' he added.

By prior agreement, they paused and waited until the others caught up; then together they walked the final mile. As the river bed gradually widened and the sand spread out before them, they began to hear the crashing of breakers. Gulls were wheeling overhead. There was salt in the air and the sun was shining. The men cheered at the sight of the sea. Now, at last, they could head for home. When they arrived at the blockhouse, however, they found that the door was locked.

'Damn Johns!' said Tostig. 'He was supposed to leave the key on the hook!'

They glanced around them. Scattered on the ground were boxes and supply cases, the majority broken open, some completely empty.

'Quite a shambles,' murmured Snaebjorn.

Guthrum took a deep breath. 'That's odd,' he remarked. 'It seems improbable, but I'd swear someone was burning coal.'

'I think you're right,' said Tostig. 'Look.'

He was pointing along the beach towards the *Centurion*.

Its tarpaulins had been removed and it was apparently occupied. Coloured bunting fluttered in the wires. The hatch was propped open, and smoke was rising from the stack.

The travellers approached.

From inside the vessel there came the sound of raucous merrymaking. A man's voice could be heard, guffawing loudly, accompanied by the giggles and squeals of several females. The portholes were all steamed up.

Tostig rapped on the hull, and instantly the laughter faded. A moment later, Cook appeared in the hatchway. He was clearly drunk, and had a half-empty spirits bottle in his hand. His demeanour was startling. His hair had grown long and was tied in a topknot. His beard was divided into a fork. He was naked apart from a loincloth, and his entire body was covered in blue decorations. Behind him were four women, similarly adorned, and also naked. For several seconds the two groups stared at each other wordlessly.

Then Tostig reached into his pocket.

Further along the beach lay *Perseverance*, which by some fortune remained untouched. A temporary camp was established in the lee of the vessel, and preparations were made to float it on the next high tide. While this work was being carried out, Tostig disappeared into the cabin and was not seen for two or three hours. When eventually he emerged his manner was subdued. He took Guthrum to one side and spoke to him in private; then he gathered his men around him.

'We are now ready to leave these shores,' he announced. 'Technically our mission has succeeded, and although it has borne no fruit we can content ourselves that we did not fail. Commander Johns, on the other hand, seems to have run into difficulties. I presume those broken boxes contained his reserve supplies; no doubt he'll be high and dry without them. He's probably marooned somewhere far from here, waiting for relief that will never come. Well, he'll get no sympathy from me. He and his followers knew exactly what they were letting themselves in for when they embarked on their expedition. Plainly, their arrangements were inadequate, based most likely on outdated preconceptions and obsolete methods. As for Johns himself, he is obviously a vain and egotistical man. It is evident that he thought of nothing else but that he should be first to arrive at the Furthest Point. I expect he had grand plans for the colony to bear his name, and to be remembered in history as the man who solved the problem of the mules. Instead of which he is lost in the wilderness, caught on the brink of starvation, and a very long way from home.'

Tostig paused and looked towards the north.

'Johns' failure is his own fault,' he said. 'Nonetheless, it is our duty to try and rescue him. Cease work on the boat. We're going back.'